BREWING TROUBLE

CHRISTINE GAEL

INTRODUCTION

After barely escaping the business end of the hangman's noose, Cricket Hawthorne wants nothing more than to forget it all...Maude the magical typewriter, Zoe's stolen cauldron, Patrick the betrayer, and definitely the witch-hating, robe-wearing cult who tried to end her. Unfortunately, pressing the reboot button isn't an option. Bringing The Crow's Feet Coven back to their former glory is her destiny, whether she likes it or not. Too bad the powers that be will do whatever it takes to stop them.

It's fight or flight, and she's never been a quitter. Now, it's up to her and her ragtag team to bring down the organization hell-bent on ridding the world of witches. But at what price?

CHAPTER 1

I DON'T KNOW how long I slept. If there were dreams, they were gone before I could commit them to memory, and the thick, inky blackness of unconsciousness was punctuated only by the aches and pains in my body and the muted sounds of voices somewhere around me. It was like I was drifting deep in a pool of water, clawing my way up for what could have been minutes, hours, or days. Eventually, though, a thread of light began to trickle in, and I began swimming to the surface.

When I finally awoke, it was with a start, my eyelids as heavy as a pair of anvils as I squinted against the light, trying to make some kind of sense of my jumbled thoughts.

It wasn't until I tried to sit up that the pain shattered the fog in my head, shooting through my torso like a lightning bolt, forcing me to suck in a raspy breath. I let out a whimper and realized that my throat was on fire. Had I gotten run over by a train or something?

Still struggling to piece together where I was, I looked around, moving gingerly so as not to upset either my stomach or my neck, and realized that I was in a bed. It wasn't my room at Mee-maw's house, but my surroundings looked eerily familiar...

I tried to prop my elbows under me, but another shaft of pain shot through my stomach, and suddenly, it all came back to me in a rush.

The kidnapping.

The cult.

The ceremony.

It felt like a bad dream, and if it weren't for the evidence of it on my body, I might have been able to convince myself that it was. But memories continued to flood my mind, and the intensity of what I had gone through over the past days was nearly enough to send me plunging back into blessed darkness.

I closed my eyes, trying to quell the panic threatening to swallow me whole as I reached down and ran my fingers over the thin line of stitches along my belly.

It had all started with that dang typewriter. Up until that day at the flea market just weeks before, my life had been that of your average middle-aged divorcee—if you didn't factor in that I was living with my grandmother and desperate to find my footing in a world where I was, once again, single, without any relevant, marketable skills to speak of. But that typewriter had given me a purpose...had awoken something inside me in the most literal sense.

Memories continued to come in bursts, and I conjured up how it felt that first time I'd sat in front of those keys. How naturally it had come to me—almost like magic.

No.

Not *like* magic.

It *had* been magic. The "stories" I'd churned out while clacking away on that old typewriter—Maude, I'd named her—which came in wild bursts of inspiration so strong that they couldn't be avoided, had all come true. Down to the smallest details, I had somehow managed to divine the future... and that was just the tip of the iceberg. What happened next had been a rollercoaster ride of research, conspiracies, break-ins, and betrayals, all culminating in the discovery that I was not only a witch, but part of a coven that likely also included my cousin, Zoe.

By the time we had finally started figuring it all out, though, our efforts had been derailed when I was taken hostage by a sect of witch hunters that had apparently existed since the colonial era—and possibly before. They had cut me open as part of some horrendous ritual, wanting to imbue Maude with my magic so that they, as non-witches, could then use her powers.

And once they'd completed their task?

They were going to hang me.

They'd nearly managed it, too. In fact, I'd been on death's door, but Zoe and Mee-maw had come to my rescue as I dangled from the noose. Only they hadn't been alone...

I froze, fresh fury washing over me in a wave as the last piece of the story clicked into place.

Patrick.

Handsome, uncannily charming, lean-hipped, hunky freaking Patrick Byrne. The Scottish handyman who had seemingly materialized out of nowhere, ready to inject some joy back into my life when it had felt like my world was coming apart at the seams. I never bothered to question his sudden appearance, or why he was so keen on spending time with me, until he was speeding down the highway with me in his car, ready to hand me over to the nutters in the cloaks with the knives. In spite of my pain and exhaustion, I could feel the anger bubbling up inside of me as I thought about his absurdly handsome face, about how close I had come to dying because of his betrayal.

And yet...

He *had* helped Mee-maw and Zoe find me, apparently. If it weren't for the bomb he'd rigged in the building, they wouldn't have gotten me out in time. That was saying something, considering that the guy's own father was the one who had tried to kill me.

My mind shot back to the very last prediction my bond with Maude had produced. Just a few short words, but they'd been chilling.

Trust only three.

Mee-maw, Zoe, and I had batted around many theories about what that meant. I knew I could trust Mee-maw and Zoe. But should that circle of trust include my high school friend Ethan, who had just come back into my life? What of Connie? And we'd also wondered if handyman Patrick was too good to be true. As much as it hurt to face now, deep down, I'd never honestly believed that he would be the one to betray me.

I'd been so wrong.

But did going back on a betrayal make up for it? I wondered as I hauled myself into a sitting position, moving agonizingly slowly so as not to upset my injuries. The last thing I could remember was the look on his face as he had climbed into the back of the car when we made our escape: worry, guilt, regret... but also a glimmer of uncertainty.

What was he to me—to us? Was he friend, foe, or something in between?

And on that note, where the hell was he, anyway? Where were Zoe and Mee-maw?

Heck...where was *I*?

I glanced around the cluttered bedroom, taking a moment to process the eggshell paint on the walls, the stained glass lamp on the bedside table, the dresser covered in knick-knacks that looked like they hadn't been dusted in years and then let out a low groan.

No. No freaking way.

As if on cue, a familiar voice boomed from the doorway, making me start.

"Hey there, Cricket. How you feeling?"

I squeezed my eyes closed for a long moment, praying for patience. If I had thought my life couldn't get any stranger, I had been wrong. Letting out a long breath, I opened my eyes and forced a tight smile.

"Not one hundred percent, if I'm being honest, Greg. How about yourself?" I croaked.

My ex-husband clomped across the floor, moving closer to stare down at me as he dumped the last of a bag of potato chips into his mouth. "Pretty a-okay, I guess," he replied around a mouthful of food, his expression unchanging.

I was sure Mee-maw and Zoe had their reasons, but in the moment, I couldn't fathom why on earth would they have brought me to the house I'd once shared with my ex-husband instead of somewhere else to recuperate like, I don't know...say, a hospital?

And what had they told him about my condition? There was no way they could've risked sharing the truth with him. Deciding to wait him out, hoping he gave me a clue, I just stared up at him expectantly.

"You've been asleep for almost sixteen hours," Greg continued, seemingly oblivious to my distress. "I was starting to get worried. That's so crazy about your stomach. I mean, you're clumsy and all, but I still don't quite understand how you managed that one." He gave a little chuckle, but his expression went serious again when he realized that I wasn't exactly seeing the levity. "How did it happen, again? I heard it from Mee-maw, but it still doesn't make a whole lot of sense."

Clearly, my family had concocted some tall tale to explain my injuries, but I still didn't have enough to go on to even fake it. My face flushed as I wracked my brain for a way out of replying. I was on the verge of pretending to faint just to avoid answering him when Zoe swept into the room.

"Ah, excellent!" she chirped, her wide eyes full of apology as she met my gaze. "You're awake. Sorry, I just left for a few minutes to take a quick shower." She reached down to gingerly touch my foot before turning to look at Greg. "I wouldn't be surprised if she doesn't remember, Greg," she hastened to add. "Cricket, remember we went for a hike and you slowed down to cut up an apple to snack on, but then you tripped on a root and fell onto your own knife?" she asked, her voice shrill as her eyes bored into mine.

Dear God, how clumsy did these people think I was that anyone would believe that? I glared at her before nodding slowly.

"Er... right," I said, glancing back up at Greg. "You know I've always been a klutz." I cleared my throat, suddenly desperate for a cold drink. "But why am I here?" I asked, looking between the two of them.

"Greg's place was way closer to where the four of us had all gone hiking. Remember, over by Bear Lake?" Zoe replied, and I could tell that she had been practicing. "We figured we could patch you up here and let you rest for a while before we made the long drive back to Mee-maw's."

Greg's brow furrowed. "Not that I mind helping you guys out, but are you sure she shouldn't go to the hospital? If you barely remember what happened, sounds like you might've hit your head, Cricket. You could have a concussion..."

Zoe opened her mouth to reply but I cut in quickly, glad to finally be able to pipe in with something useful. "You *do* recall that I'm only working part time right now, right, Greg? And you took me off your medical insurance plan last week, even though you agreed to keep me on. A hospital bill would've been thousands of dollars that I don't have, because we still haven't been able to sell this house yet."

Apparently, I didn't need to remind him that was *also* his fault as he went beet red, looking down at the floor and shuffling his feet.

"Right," he muttered, "well, to be fair, you never go to the doctor so the insurance thing seemed like a waste. I was pretty sure you wouldn't even notice. I'll call about the insurance thing and see if I can get you back on for the next few months, though. And, um, since you're laid up, I'll contact the real estate agent and see what we can do to get that rolling again, too." Zoe shot him a raised brow and he looked away, crumpling his empty chip bag in his hand. "In the meantime, you guys can stay as long as you need to, Cricket. Don't even worry about it..." Without another word, he scurried out of the room, leaving me and Zoe alone.

"Thank you, Greg," I called after him. Greg and his inability to manage life in general was a big part of the reason I had left, but that might actually benefit me for a change. At least if I kept him on the defensive, he was less likely to start thinking too hard about our extremely thin excuse for being camped out at his house right now.

Zoe and I just stared at each other, motionless and silent until his footsteps had faded completely. She moved to perch on the side of the bed, reaching into her pocket and pulling out three aspirin. She handed them to me, followed by the glass of water on the bedside table. I took the pills and washed them down as she leaned closer.

"Well, that was a close one," she whispered. "I swear, I was by your side the whole dang time to make sure that didn't happen, and you were knocked out like a light. Then, I walk away for a bit to cook and shower, in he comes to—"

"What the hell is going on?" I hissed. "Greg's right! Why

didn't you guys take me to the hospital? And who the hell stitched me up?"

The sound of a throat clearing had us both swinging our gazes to the doorway, where Mee-maw and Patrick were now standing. Patrick's eyes found mine for a moment, and another muddled memory hit me like a freight train. The Scotsman convincing me, through blood, deliriousness, and agony, to let *him* stitch me up.

And I'd agreed.

It was weird how I didn't remember the actual process hurting, in spite of the pain I had been in. He must have been very gentle, but I shoved the thought away before I could dwell any further. Mee-maw and Patrick exchanged a glance as he took a tentative step closer to the bed.

"We thought about it, Cricket, we really did," he said in a low voice. "But if we'd taken you to a hospital, they would have called the cops due to the knife wound. I know you're pissed at me, and you have every reason to be, but I think we can all agree having the police involved is not a complication we can afford right now."

"As the person who was kidnapped, stabbed and strung up, I think I should've had a say in that," I muttered miserably.

"What would we have told them?" Mee-maw asked, crossing her arms. "That the witch Illuminati stole your magical typewriter?"

Well, when she put it that way...

"Patrick's right, Cricket," Zoe chimed in with a grim nod. "We needed to stay under the radar and bring you somewhere safe—no hotels with a paper trail leading the enemy to us, no plane tickets. Whatever we do next, we're going to have to lay low and strategize. The last thing any of us want is for those guys to make another play for you. Not until you're feeling better, and we're armed with more knowledge about how this all works and how deep this web of evil goes."

"We didn't have a lot of time or a lot of options," Mee-maw added defensively.

There was a long moment of silence before I let out a sigh and tipped my head in a curt nod. "I get that," I said as I shot a glance toward the door. "But we can't stay long. What if my kids show up? They visit Greg at least once a week. I don't want them involved in this—ever. It's bad enough that I dragged the two of you into it." I glanced between Zoe and Mee-maw, deliberately avoiding Patrick's gaze. "We need to figure out another plan, ASAP."

Zoe blew out a pent-up breath. "Crap. I didn't even think of the kids. I didn't realize they saw Greg so often since they hardly even call y--" She caught herself and cleared her throat. "Um, since I know how busy they are with their own lives right now. But I'm with you. We can't put them at risk. I know this is going to sound crazy, but what about finding some kind of a safehouse in Rocky Knoll?"

Patrick opened his mouth to protest but Zoe pushed on.

"Running isn't going to cut it. They will go to the ends of the earth to find us, so until we figure out how to use the magical items and take a stand, we'll be in constant danger. If we hide in or near Rocky Knoll we can do surveillance on Connie and spend our time researching the Crow's Feet Coven history, where it apparently originated," Zoe suggested. "We just need a base of operations, somewhere with no ties to any of us that we can rent for cash. I have some hidden in one of the freezers at the bakery for emergencies, and this definitely qualifies."

"We are good for cash," Patrick interjected. "I have some stashed, as well."

"I can start looking on the apocalypse prepper message boards for bunkers and the like in our area," Mee-maw volunteered. "It might not be pretty, but I think I can find something within the next day or two that will work well enough."

"Okay," I said, still ignoring Patrick as I directed my attention to Mee-maw, a new question suddenly at the front of my mind as my fingertips began to tingle. "What about Maude... where is my typewriter?" I asked hesitantly.

"Fine," Mee-maw assured me. "It's in the car. I put it in the back seat, with a blanket over it. Door's locked and the alarm is on."

I nodded, relief washing over me. It had become so much more than a conduit for magic since I had bought it, practically coming to take on a life of its own. The thought of it falling into the wrong hands again made my stomach turn.

I finally met Patrick's gaze, my expression hardening as I stared him down. I wished the others were gone so I could lay into him about everything—why he had turned me in, why he had changed his mind, what his endgame was... but one look at Mee-maw was enough to tell me that now wasn't the time. My grandmother's face already looked drawn and pale, and considering her recent heart attack and the past few days, she hardly needed any additional pressure.

Just then, my stomach gave a rumble loud enough to make everyone turn and stare at me. If what Greg had said was right, it had been more than a day since I had last eaten. Food suddenly felt like the only thing that mattered right now.

Zoe pushed herself to her feet with a half-smile. "I've already got a meal ready, if you guys are hungry. It's a bit early for dinner, but I figured you'd be starving by the time you woke up, Cricket."

"You're a genius."

"I can bring you up a plate, if you want--" Zoe began, but I was already shaking my head.

"No," I replied. "I've been in bed long enough. It would be good for me to stretch my legs, I think."

I shoved the blankets aside, relieved but somewhat surprised to find I was dressed in clean jogging pants and a hoodie.

"You were covered in blood so we stopped at Walmart and grabbed you some clothes," Zoe said, holding out both hands to me and helping me get to my feet as the others filed out of the room. I took a second to lean into her.

"Thanks. And thanks for rescuing me. That was a close one," I murmured. "I was so afraid they'd caught you, too...that-_"

I broke off as tears clogged my achy throat.

"I'm fine. We're both fine, okay?" she said, squeezing my hands more tightly. "Now get it together, Crick, because we have to keep it that way."

I nodded and sucked in a shuddering breath. She was right. We were safe for the moment, but we'd only cleared the first hill. There was still a mountain in front of us to conquer. I could fall apart later...if we survived.

Pushing that thought aside, I straightened, which seemed to ease the pain in my torso. After a couple of wobbly moments, I was able to make it to the first floor with my cousin's assistance.

I hobbled into the dining room to find Patrick had a chair pulled out for me. He laid a steadying hand on my lower back as I gingerly slipped into the seat. Dimly, I noted Greg watching, his brow furrowing in suspicion as the muscular handyman took a seat beside me. Greg glanced down and sucked in his own stomach before giving a derisive sniff and reaching for the nearest tray. The rest of us followed suit and dug in. As awkward as the situation was, it might just have been the best dang food I had ever eaten.

Fried chicken with buttery, flaky biscuits and mashed potatoes. Green beans gleaming with olive oil, and a fresh, green salad topped off our feast. In spite of the pain in my stomach, I found it nearly impossible to stop eating. The whole time I stuffed my face, though, I was aware of the fireworks between Greg and Patrick, which went beyond contemptuous looks; they both seemed eager to help me get whatever I needed, nearly tripping over themselves to keep my glass full and the dishes within reach. At one point, I caught a glimpse of Greg flexing his non-existent biceps as he reached for the tray of chicken again and I had to struggle not to roll my eyes. He'd never given a crap about impressing me when we were married. Heck, he'd barely even noticed when I was in the room, and now he was suddenly trying to impress me?

Men.

When we'd finally finished our food, Zoe excused herself to take a call from her husband, Phil, who was out of town on business, per usual. I had no idea what she was going to tell him about this whole mess, but surely he'd be in danger if he went back to their house after his trip?

I was still wondering how Zoe was going to handle that conundrum when Mee-maw piped up.

"Greg," she said, shooting me a glance from across the table, "how about you and I clean up some of these dishes?"

Greg looked like he wanted to protest, but the no-nonsense expression on my grandmother's face stopped him short. He stiffly got to his feet, taking one last glance at Patrick before collecting an armful of plates and walking out of the room. Mee-maw followed him into the kitchen, leaving me and Patrick alone in silence.

Despite a full belly and the aspirin taking the edge off my pain, I could already feel myself getting angry again. I opened my mouth, ready to rip him a new one, but he raised a hand to stop me.

"Before you say anything," he said, sounding like he was

choosing his words carefully, "there's something you need to know, Cricket."

"Do tell," I shot back with a raw chuckle. "Is it about how you were just using me this whole time? How your dad is the leader of some insane sect of witch-hunters hell-bent on murdering me? Heck, why stop there? Is Patrick Byrne really even your name?"

His lips thinned and he inclined his head. "I understand that you're angry," he said, "and you have every right to be. I'll tell you everything I know and you can ream me out once we leave this place and have more time alone. But there's something I need to tell you that I haven't spoken to the others about."

I swallowed hard, my hands balling into fists under the table. Part of me wanted to tell him to stuff it where the sun didn't shine, but the other part remembered the guilt on his face back in the car.

"Fine. What is it?"

"Look, magical abilities like this...they aren't random," he said carefully. "Witch powers tend to be hereditary, which means that covens are often family-based." He cleared his throat, meeting my gaze. "You and Zoe both have the gift. You have Maude as your conduit, and we have to assume the cauldron is hers," he continued. "Covens are comprised of at least three witches, not including the Everlasting Conservator. Now, I can't say for sure, but I think it's pretty clear who the third is—the one you need to make up your coven of three and bring you all into your full power eventually. Are...Are you following me, Cricket?"

"Who's down for some 'nanner splits?" The sound of Meemaw's booming voice in the doorway pulled my attention away from him, and I turned to see her scrutinizing us from under her helmet of steely gray hair, overflowing bowls of ice cream in hand.

My eyes went wide as I turned back to face Patrick, the whole world seeming to grind to a halt around us.

"Holy schnikeys, y'all look like you just saw a Sasquatch. What gives?"

What "gave" was that, not only were my cousin and I both witches being hunted down like dogs, but if Patrick was right? Our octogenarian, conspiracy theory-loving grandmother was one, too.

God help us all.

CHAPTER 2

"Is it just me, or was Greg making eyes at you back over dinner?" asked Zoe, downing the last of the iced tea in her glass and leaning back in the glider. She gave me a pointed look, and I shook my head.

"Come on," I muttered, avoiding her eyes and taking a sip of my own tea. "You're seeing things."

"Nuh-uh," Mee-maw butted in from her rocker in the corner of the porch. "Zoe's right, Cricket. He was climbing you like a tree. Except with his eyes."

"Mee-maw!" I protested, flushing a little. "Greg's just one of those people who only wants what he can't have. I could remarry him tomorrow and by Friday he'd be treating me like a piece of furniture again."

Mee-maw muttered something under her breath, glancing over her shoulder back into the darkened kitchen. Greg had spent most of his time after dinner watching TV in the living room while Mee-maw, Patrick and Zoe had played Scrabble. I'd passed on game night under the pretense of lying down again, but I hadn't been feeling tired. I'd just wanted some time to process everything. So much had happened so quickly, I'd been too distracted to really think about the crone's coven lore once Zoe had stolen the cauldron, what with being kidnapped and nearly murdered, but now it was all I could think about. I'd spent hours pacing in my room, wishing I could go get Maude to see if she could help. But surely if I was spotted lugging it in, Greg would wonder why I'd gone hiking and brought a massive typewriter along with me.

More than that, though? I wasn't ready to reunite with old Maude yet. Something had happened during the ceremony. Something bad, that I still didn't feel strong enough to face quite yet. I could still sense her presence...still feel the pull of her teasing my fingertips, but the urgency? The crazed need to type and that pulsing thread between us?

It was gone.

"Factum."

The word echoed in my mind even as my stomach wound throbbed. Memories assailed me in an all-consuming rush. The prison guard and the pain he'd wrought with his necklace from hell. Finneas standing over me, chanting words he forced me to repeat under the threat of Mee-maw's life. Me, parroting them in a daze of pain and terror. The keen slice of the blade, and blood splattering out onto my typewriter. Our bond trembling...stretching...the fibers snapping, one by one, each occasion a fresh agony until all that remained were a few thin, gossamer strands connecting us. Then, sickly green lightning filling the room as power crackled in the air. The cultists had cheered, dragging me roughly to the gallows, forcing my head through the noose--

I swallowed a strangled cry, sweat popping out on my upper lip as I shoved the memories aside. Replaying that trauma could do me no good. Not now, at least. Maybe someday, I could relive it and try to work through it. But first on my to-do list? Keep it from happening again. To me. To Zoe. And, apparently, to Mee-maw.

I was still reeling from the bombshell Patrick had dropped on me. I didn't know where he was right now, and frankly, I didn't care; I still hadn't gotten my head around his theory about Mee-maw. And as much as I hated listening to the others speculate about Greg's feelings for me, the only thing I would rather do less was tell them Mee-maw was likely a witch, too.

It made a horrible kind of sense, especially if witchy powers were genetic, as Patrick had affirmed, but that was one can of worms I wasn't ready to open yet. We barely had any idea how my own powers worked, much less how to properly harness them. And Zoe had only just discovered an attachment to the cauldron she had found at Connie's place the evening I'd been kidnapped. The last thing we needed right now was Mee-maw trying to alakazam things when we didn't know for sure she was a witch—*or* what her magical item might be if she *was* part of the coven.

Deep down, I knew that the issue wasn't going to go away, and that I would have to address it sooner or later, but we had bigger fish to fry right now. The others seemed to know it, too, and I watched as Zoe's expression turned serious and she cleared her throat.

"Enough about Greg. We need to talk about Lizzie and Jack..."

I leaned forward, pinching the bridge of my nose. Right before going to bed, Greg had delivered some news that had made my stomach drop: the kids were coming to visit him tomorrow, and that meant we needed to be as far away from here as humanly possible. It wasn't that I didn't want to see them; on the contrary, spending some time with them would probably have been just what the doctor ordered. But the risk to their safety was too great. Sure, I was still a little bitter that they had rallied behind Greg in the aftermath of our divorce, but they were my kids. *Our* kids. And I loved them more than life itself. The divorce couldn't have been easy on them, and I knew that they weren't intentionally taking sides. Still, the fact that they seemed to be coming over to Greg's place every weekend when I hadn't seen hide nor hair of them since moving in with Mee-maw had hurt.

"Cricket?"

I started when I realized Zoe had asked me something and was waiting for a response. "Sorry," I said, blinking. "What was that?"

"I know you're worried about the kids. I am, too, but I doubt Finneas and his posse would be able to find us here that fast. Maybe we could stick around just another day or two?" Zoe exchanged a look with Mee-maw, who gave a grim nod. "I'm no doctor, but I think you could use some more time to heal."

"You don't need to be a doctor to have common sense," Mee-maw said. "That Finneas guy damn near carved you up like a Thanksgiving turkey. You need bed rest, not a road trip."

"Nope," I replied, crossing my arms. "No way. That's not even a discussion."

"Cricket," Zoe began, reaching out to touch my arm, "I really think that you should consider--"

"No," I insisted, and could feel my jaw setting. "We all have targets on our backs, and I don't want to put the kids in the line of fire, too." I shook my head. "We're leaving before they get here, and that's final. We can figure out the rest later. And besides..." I glanced down at my stomach, which was still tender and inflamed to the touch, but not nearly as bad as I'd have expected. Patrick was clearly a skilled nurse. "I feel better after some rest and a good meal."

"Actually, you feel better because of your magic," came a low voice from the back door. I turned to see Patrick pulling it slowly shut before coming to stand in front of us, his hands on his lean hips. His dark hair was damp and curly from the shower he'd just taken, and I found myself struggling not to ogle his toned torso under his threadbare t-shirt.

"What are you saying?" I asked him, confused. "That I'm healing myself, somehow? I haven't even touched Maude since-"

"It's not specific to you and has nothing to do with your conduit, except that you had that initial connection with it," Patrick replied. "It's an aspect of witch powers in general. Once they've been awoken by the bond with your magical item, your body slowly changes. You'll get sick less often, enjoy heightened vitality, and—ideally—live longer. You'll also heal faster than a normal person."

"Like a superhero," Zoe said, clapping excitedly. "Nice."

I put a hand to my throat beneath the collar of my hoodie, where a faint, yellowing ring of bruises from the noose still remained. Seemingly on the same wavelength, Patrick nodded, meeting my gaze.

"Most people wouldn't be up and about the day after being hanged," he said, "or stabbed, for that matter. I'm willing to bet that your neck will be fine by tomorrow morning, and in another few days, your stomach will be like new."

Mee-maw startled me by bursting out into high-spirited laughter, slapping her knee. "Well, butter my butt and call me a biscuit," she exclaimed. "That's not too shabby of a side effect, Cricket!"

"No," I agreed, chewing my lip in thought. "It's not." It made sense, though. In the few hours since getting up, I had already started to feel better, to the point where I could walk around unaided. It was an interesting change of pace from the old days—three weeks ago—when sleeping the wrong way could have me feeling creaky and sore all day.

"Does this mean no more wrinkles?" Zoe asked, an excited gleam in her eye. "Not that it's important in the scheme of things, but just curious," she rushed to explain.

"To my knowledge, your skin will age more slowly, along with the rest of your body, but any wrinkles there now will remain," Patrick replied, barely sparing her a glance as he took a tentative step toward me, indicating the space beside me. "Do you mind if I sit with you?" he asked.

I hesitated but then sighed and nodded, scooting to the left to make room for him. He settled in, his jean-clad leg brushing up against mine, and I found myself stiffening at his touch.

"Cricket's right," he said, running a hand through his damp hair. "It's risky to leave, but if we stay here, it's only a matter of time before they show up. I'm not willing to gamble. Not now, when I've seen up close and personal what they're capable of. If you don't want your kids involved, then we need to leave before they get here. The Organization has deep pockets. Their connections are widespread, and their resources are practically limitless. They'll have probably taken a day or so to regroup after we set off the bomb, but make no mistake: they *will* find this place if we stay."

Mee-maw snorted. "'The Organization'?" she said. "I guess they realized how stupid the Illuminati sounded, huh?"

Patrick gave her a thin smile. "Maybe," he replied. "Although, I'm pretty sure the Illuminati doesn't exist. The Organization, on the other hand...they are very real, and very dangerous."

"What's this *'they'* stuff? Don't you mean *'you'*?" I asked, shooting him a glare. "I mean, you *were* working for them...or have we all just suddenly forgotten about that?"

Patrick sighed, rubbing his hands over his knees before

responding. "I won't make excuses for my father or his acolytes," he began, choosing his words carefully. "But being the leader of the Organization is a heavy burden, and it's easy to scapegoat the group that's trying to keep order."

"Keep order?" Mee-maw asked incredulously. "Since when do kidnapping, hanging, and voodoo count as 'keeping order'?"

Patrick grimaced. "They don't," he acknowledged, "and that wasn't the original mission of the group...it certainly wasn't *my* mission. But you need to understand that despite all the romanticizing of witches in folklore and movies, they have historically caused a great deal of pain and trouble." I bristled at that, but he pressed on. "Try to imagine what it was like centuries ago," he said. "The terror of having a curse put on you. Being coerced into doing things you didn't want to do, by unseen forces. Some witches started plagues, used black magic, caused natural disasters..." His muscular throat worked as he caught and held my gaze. "The Organization wasn't always what it is today. Its original purpose—my reason for staying— was to make sure that no one could use magic to subjugate or hurt anyone else. Clearly, the balance has shifted."

"Lovely," I muttered, shaking my head. "So now they've become the very thing they fought against, is that it?"

Patrick didn't meet my eyes as he spoke, his voice going quiet. "It's ugly," he said, "but a lot of people would say that that oversight was necessary at points. That's probably hard for you to believe, but it's true. I'm not going to make excuses for what happened to you, Cricket. There *is* no excuse, and that's why I stepped in. But not everyone is like you. The type of power that comes with magic can...change people in ways you can't even imagine. Trust me on that."

I peered over at him in the dim light of the porch, searching for any signs of dishonesty, but I found none. Whether what he was saying was true or not, *he* believed it. His face was drawn, his eyes had gone dark, and he looked like he wanted to say more but couldn't bring himself to.

"So what's your dad's true role in all this?" Zoe asked. "What does he do...aside from torture innocent women, that is."

Patrick cleared his throat. "Initially, it was just to stop witches from uniting with their items. The idea was that if we could keep them separate, witches' powers would never awaken, and that would be that. No one would get hurt on either side and eventually magic would die out after centuries of lying dormant." I let out a snort of protest at that, but said nothing. "But he got greedy," Patrick continued. "He and the rest became convinced that magic could help them protect humanity, and that they could do more good with it than the witches had. They figured that if it were wielded by someone in a controlled setting, and there were checks and balances in place--"

"Ha!" Mee-maw cackled. "Sounds about right—of course men want to steal power from women. They can do it better, right?"

Patrick nodded grimly. "You're not wrong," he admitted. "It's so clear to me now. You have to understand that I was brought up to think that witches were evil, preying on innocent people, drunk on their own power. And everything I'd been shown and taught supported that theory. Until..." His eyes flickered over to me for just a moment, but he cleared his throat and pressed on. "I don't think my father started out as a bad person," he said, "but the truth is that he's been corrupted by the promise of power himself. He can't be trusted to do what's right. Not anymore."

I stared at him for a long moment before asking, "What about you, Patrick?" It was time to draw a line in the sand and see which side Patrick Byrne landed on. We needed to know that he was in—*all* in—with us and our cause, or whether he still had reservations.

He looked at me with an earnestness that left me feeling taken aback. "You're not evil, Cricket. I can't be sure of many things, but I know that much is true. Magic is a scary thing, though." He shrugged his broad shoulders. "I guess I've just finally realized that it's here for a reason. It has a purpose. And it's not up to me or the Organization to decide what that purpose is."

"Whose decision is it, then?" I asked, my body tingling with something like hope as I waited for his answer.

He met my gaze and held it. "Yours and those like you. Witches. Trying to punish someone for a crime before it's happened isn't the way to do it. If a witch wields her power for evil, then yes, I believe there should be an organization to protect the weaker faction of humanity and find a way to stop it. But to strip a body of their birthright when they've committed no crime?" He set his jaw. "That's wrong. There's no doubt about it." His light brogue had grown thicker as he grew more impassioned, and I couldn't deny, he was compelling as all get out. He shot to his feet and stared down at the three of us. "And it's a tyranny that won't continue. Not on my watch. You don't have to accept my help, but that won't stop me from trying to dismantle the Organization and take my father down. I just think we'd be stronger as a team."

It was a pretty speech. But, dang, he'd hurt me. My pride, my ability to trust...it would be a long time before I'd forget what he'd done.

I glanced from Zoe to Mee-maw. They seemed to be waiting for me to make the call. "There's something I still don't get," I said slowly, addressing Patrick. He waited for me to go on. "The man who broke in and stole my typewriter. My jailer said he tried to get Maude for himself and--"

"That's true. He was a low-level member of the Organization," Patrick said, anticipating my question. "From what I've gathered, his wife was terminally ill. He heard about the power of the typewriter and he thought he could use it to help her."

That rocked me back on my heels some as I imagined the poor man's feelings of helplessness.

"And the hit and run?" I prompted, ignoring the sudden ache in my throat. "He was hit by a black sedan. The same kind you were driving when you brought me to your father, Patrick."

He held his hands up. "I had nothing to do with that, Cricket. You have to believe me. I still don't know what happened, exactly, but there's a standard issue vehicle for members of the Organization." Seeing my skepticism, he continued, "As soon as I saw that newscast, I went straight to my father. He told me they went after him to get the typewriter, and there was a chase as he tried to get away on foot. When the guy realized there was no escape, he veered in front of the car. There was no avoiding him." Patrick scrubbed a hand over his face. "I know it sounds weak. When I think back on it all, there were so many red flags that I ignored. But up until then, I'd never even been able to imagine my father hurting someone, never mind ordering their death. I've finally accepted the truth, though. He probably had that guy murdered. My father is off the deep end and he needs to be stopped, at all costs."

My heart skipped a beat at the solemn resolve in his eyes.

"Most people can't see that kind of thing, even when it's right in front of their face," Mee-maw observed quietly.

He was breathing hard, looking between the three of us and waiting for a response. "We could use the help, Cricket," Zoe murmured. "And who knows more about the inner workings of the Organization than Patrick?"

I sighed, meeting Patrick's gaze. "We don't have much of a

choice but to trust you. I'm not saying I forgive you...but I'll accept your help. For now, anyway."

Patrick tipped his head in a grim nod. "Brilliant," he said. "Then I guess I'll start by telling you that I think I have the perfect place for us to hide out."

CHAPTER 3

"The *library*?" I said, staring at the building in the distance before rounding on Patrick, who stood a few yards away, hands in pockets. "The *public* library?"

Truth be told, it was my bad. When Patrick had said he had a place in Rocky Knoll for us to hide out for the next few days, I'd spent the drive over more concerned with the fact that he'd used the term "us"—i.e., including him—than I'd been about the actual location. When I'd accepted his help, I hadn't really considered that we'd all be holed up together, sleeping in the same space. Then, when I finally did start to think about the potential options for our safehouse, I'd imagined a clandestine cabin where we could be close to the action and keep tabs on the Organization while Zoe figured out how to use her magic and I tried to reconnect with Maude.

A public building in the center of town that had people in and out all day hardly fit the bill.

"Kinda ballsy, even for me," Mee-maw said as she squinted at the building in the darkness.

We had parked down a nearby alleyway, but there had been

no need. It was two AM and the place was like a ghost town. Tomorrow, though, Main Street would be buzzing with activity.

"We won't be hiding out *in* the library," Patrick corrected as he tugged a key ring from his pocket. "We'll be hiding *under* it. There is a virtual catacomb of unused rooms in the basement at our disposal, including a bathroom. Trudy gave me the keys to the building, allowing me to go in and do the noisiest work before they opened and after closing to keep from disturbing the patrons. There is still a laundry list of repairs that need doing, so they won't be asking for the keys back anytime soon."

I chewed on my lower lip, still not convinced.

"You need to understand that no matter where we are, the Organization is going to find us. We're buying time to collect information, at this point. Let's get you all settled in and then I'll go hit up my cash reserves and head over to Mannington to the 24-hour Walmart."

We'd stopped off and pooled our change and errant dollar bills to get some waters and snacks at a convenience store, but we definitely needed some supplies.

"I'll grab some clothes but also a laptop, and some stuff to sleep on. We'll be fine, "Patrick added.

I mulled that over, trying not to focus on the "stuff to sleep on" part, and eventually nodded. He knew better than I did, and at this point, with no better alternative at hand, the point was moot. "Okay, I guess we'll make it work. And for now, it's all we've got." The idea of camping out under a public building still didn't sit entirely right with me, but what was the old saying about hiding in plain sight? As long as Patrick had the only set of keys, it might be a good option for the time being. The last thing we needed was some night janitor stumbling across a coven of witches camping out in the library basement.

"Mee-maw, what about your heart medication and such?"

I turned to see her fumbling in her enormous granny

satchel. "Got 'em right here. Even got some Metamucil. Never leave home without it," she said with a grin, holding the bottle up proudly. "Also," she added, hauling out an enormous laptop and slapping it affectionately, "no need for the laptop, Patrick. I've got that part taken care of."

I squinted at the computer, my eyes going wide with recognition a split second later. "Mee-maw, is that *Greg's?*" I hissed. "Did you steal Greg's laptop?"

Mee-maw gave a derisive sniff. "That ding dong doesn't know how to use it, anyways. You know, Cricket, I never spent a whole lot of time alone with the guy when you two were together, but after the past 24 hours, I'm starting to understand why you left him."

"That doesn't make it okay to steal," I protested, even though I was secretly pleased by the latter part of her reply. She'd been of the "divorce is rarely an option" mindset and had come down on me pretty hard when I'd left Greg. Hearing that she finally got it...even a little, was a balm to my battered heart. "What if he misses it?"

Mee-maw waved a dismissive hand at me. "Relax. You could steal his shoes off his damned feet and he wouldn't notice."

Zoe stifled a laugh at that, and I shot her a look even as I struggled not to smile myself. Patrick padded over to the car and yanked open the back door, pulling Maude off the seat. The old girl was still covered in a blanket, which suited me fine for now—there was a painful reunion coming, but now wasn't the time for it. I felt a surge of protectiveness watching him carry the typewriter—a bit like a new mom letting someone hold her baby—but Maude was heavy, and there was no way I would manage carrying her on my own right now, witchy healing abilities or no.

"Well, what are we waiting for?" Mee-maw asked, coming to stand beside me. "We're burning moonlight."

Without another word, the four of us began to skulk out of the alleyway, locking the car and leaving it behind. I felt a little like a criminal, glancing nervously this way and that as we crossed the street and into the empty parking lot.

"Move in a zigzag pattern, just in case," Mee-maw muttered, shooting a glare up at one of the flickering street lamps. "We're pretty exposed here." She rushed to the front of our ragtag group, moving in a serpentine pattern as she stole furtive glances around.

She's enjoying this, I realized, shaking my head in disbelief. This was her chance to finally live out that Mission Impossible fantasy. The three of us trailed behind her in a straight line, our footsteps echoing softly on the asphalt as we crept toward the large, brick building. I was about to step up onto the sidewalk when Mee-maw shot an arm out to stop me, nearly knocking me over. Her eyes were as big as saucers.

"Halt!"

"Jeez, Mee-maw, what?" I hissed, heart hammering in my chest.

"Don't move," she whispered back. "I heard something."

Patrick and I looked at each other, the four of us remaining frozen in place while Mee-maw put her arms out like a cartoon character, eyes narrow with suspicion. "Mee-maw," Zoe began, "are you sure--"

"Shh!" Mee-maw hissed, her head snapping back and forth. She reminded me of an old hound dog that had just caught the scent of its prey. There was a long moment of silence as we waited for her to say something. I was on the verge of starting to walk again when Mee-maw suddenly yelped and lunged to the side, shoving me out of the way like a bomb had gone off. Pain rocketed through my side as a shadow crossed in front of one of the light posts, looking long and monstrous... and then it shrank again as the stray cat that had cast it padded across the sidewalk and disappeared under the bushes.

"Seriously?" I gasped, pressing a hand to my throbbing stomach and turning to Mee-maw.

"How was I supposed to know it was a cat?" she replied, straightening her jacket with a huff. "It could have been an assassin. Forgive me for watching your six."

I rolled my eyes, but Patrick bit back a smile and jerked his head toward the building steps.

"Let's keep moving."

Still a little on edge, we scurried the rest of the way to the library entrance in silence, pausing on the steps as Patrick set Maude down and fished his keyring out of his pocket. He had to squint in the darkness while he found the one he needed, leaving the rest of us to wait and shuffle our feet. After several agonizing seconds, he located the key and unlocked the front door, holding it open for us as we filed into the empty building one by one.

It was hard to make much out as we picked our way through the darkness, and at one point I smacked into the edge of the circulation desk, letting out a string of curse words. Moonlight filtered in through the broad glass windows, and our eyes slowly began to adjust as we headed down the long hallway past the children's section. As much as I hated to admit it, I was glad to feel Patrick's sturdy presence beside me—our past interactions aside, he gave off an air of calm reassurance that I appreciated more than I liked.

Somehow, we made it to the back hallway and waited as Patrick unlocked the door to the restricted rooms.

"The employee lounge is through here," he murmured as we filed into the corridor. "The door to the basement is in the back. All we have to do is..."

He trailed off and we all stopped in our tracks as Patrick

threw up a staying hand. There, just yards away, stood a lanky figure silhouetted against the back wall of windows. My heart jumped to my throat and I was about to instruct everyone to run when Mee-maw muscled forward.

"Don't move!" she bellowed, pulling a revolver out of her granny satchel. "Put your hands where I can see them!" The sound of a gun cocking reverberated through the silence, and her eyes flashed in the darkness.

"Put the gun away. It's just a coat rack!" Patrick hurried past her and towards the dark silhouette, tugging the jacket off the top to reveal an old-fashioned coat tree leaning against the far wall. "Someone must have left this here," he said, letting the jacket that had been hanging fall to the ground. I closed my eyes for a moment, taking a deep breath as my heart rate slowly returned to normal.

"Mee-maw, jeez…why are you packing heat?" I demanded, reaching out and pushing her wrist down. "What if that had been an innocent person?"

"Relax," Mee-maw said, tucking the gun into the elastic waistband of her jeans like a cop in an old movie. "It's not loaded."

I glared at her for a moment, only slightly mollified.

A few, blessedly uneventful, minutes later, we made it down the stairs and into the lower level, which turned out to be as Patrick had described, a veritable labyrinth of old storage rooms and archives that looked like they hadn't been used in years. He paused by the base of the stairs to flip on a light switch, and the fluorescent bulbs overhead flickered to life, casting the basement in a gloomy pallor. A layer of dust covered just about every surface, and the air was stale and stagnant, but it seemed like it would work. Definitely not a heavily trafficked area.

"Do we still get Wi-Fi down here?" Mee-maw asked as Patrick led us down the hallway.

"We should," Patrick replied. "The server room sits directly above us and the library has excellent Wi-Fi due to the size of the building and amount of use."

"Good," said Mee-maw, nodding her approval. "Then I think this will do, then."

We watched as Patrick pushed open a door on the left, which led into one of the more spacious rooms on the floor. Aside from some old chairs, a stack of magazines in the corner, and a rickety old table, it was empty.

"I was thinking we could camp out here," Patrick suggested as we filed in.

Zoe leaned gingerly on the table while Mee-maw settled into one of the chairs. She sneezed twice and then popped open Greg's laptop, seemingly content with the digs.

"I'm going to head to the store and start stocking up on essentials," Patrick continued. "Let me know what you want me to pick up."

"I'll need a white board," Mee-maw told him, "along with yarn, tape, printer paper, and dry erase markers." I fought the urge to roll my eyes. She was clearly going to recreate the conspiracy board she had in her bedroom, but who was I to complain? It had come in handy last time.

Zoe opened her rucksack and withdrew the cauldron she had found at Connie's, holding it reverently. It was clear that she'd already formed some sort of bond with the item. "Do you think we should try to get some sort of potion ingredients?" she asked as she stared at it as if it were the most beautiful thing she'd ever seen. "Maybe now would be a good time to try to figure out how it works."

"I hate to say it, Zoe, but I'm pretty sure Walmart won't sell eye of newt or toad's breath," I said. "Maybe we should have Mee-maw do some research on the potions front, first. I'm making jokes here, but for all I know, potions can be made with saffron and Splenda nowadays."

"You're probably right," Zoe replied with a nod, glancing over at our grandmother.

"I'm on it!" Mee-maw said, already tapping away at the computer. "That dum-dum doesn't even have this thing password protected. It's like a free for all in here."

"All right, then, I'm going to head out," Patrick said, nodding. "I'll also get some food and bedding. We may end up being here for a while."

"How long will you be gone?" I asked him, crossing my arms.

"Few hours, give or take," he responded. "I want to hide the car on a trail in the woods afterward, which is going to take some time. I'll be back, though—I promise." His eyes met mine, and I resisted the urge to tell him to be careful. He wasn't my boyfriend—heck, he wasn't even my *friend*, at this point. We had to work together for now, and that was it. Biting the inside of my cheek, I gave him a curt nod, watching as he turned and headed out the door.

"Well," Zoe said, walking over to me as she gingerly set the cauldron down, "what now?"

"We might as well try to tidy this place up a bit," I suggested. "Mee-maw can research while we try to make this as comfortable as possible."

Zoe nodded, and together we made our way around the room, picking up errant trash, moving the chairs out of the way, and brushing away the cobwebs and dust with some old rags we'd found. We finished by setting the typewriter and cauldron side by side on the table, and I was astonished at how right they looked sitting next to one another.

The familiar pull towards the typewriter tugged at me, and my fingers tingled, but it was different than it had been before the ritual. It felt...removed, somehow—torn, like there were miles between us instead of feet. Swallowing hard, I took a few slow steps over to it, running my hands gently over the old keys. What struck me was a sense of grief and loss, so intense that it threatened to overwhelm me completely.

"Factum."

The word reverberated in my mind again, and despite not knowing what language it stemmed from, the deepest part of me knew what it represented. I still hadn't told any of them yet. I could barely face it myself.

Whatever deed they'd done, intending to break the bond between Maude and I, had definitely had an effect. Something between us was very wrong.

And I had no idea how to make it right.

CHAPTER 4

"What about this one?" Mee-maw asked, jabbing a finger toward something on Greg's computer screen.

"Mee-maw, for the love of God," said Zoe, rubbing a hand over her face, "when you said you were going to research potions, we were hoping you'd focus on something more useful in mind than one for my libido. Which is fine, in case anyone needed to know."

Mee-maw held her hands up defensively. "Look, I'm just trying to work with what we've got. We're not exactly pros, here!"

"Which is exactly why we shouldn't be trying to make potions like…that, yet. Start with something simple."

I watched with an amused grin as they continued their banter, hunched over the computer in search of beginner potion recipes. I was perched on a chair in the far corner of the room, my hands in my lap, my eyes occasionally flickering over to Maude on the table. I had spent the previous couple hours trying to type something on Maude—anything—but the familiar inspiration that signaled one of my special stories never struck.

Instead, there was just that hollow, mournful feeling I had felt earlier when I touched her, and it scared me.

As much as I wanted to just give my body some more rest and time to heal while we waited for Patrick to return, I had realized something as I listened to Zoe and Mee-maw bicker, and now it wouldn't leave me alone. For the past day or so, the hot flashes I had been feeling for the past several weeks hadn't been appearing nearly as much. Under normal circumstances, that would've been great. Who wanted to feel like they'd swallowed a nuclear bomb and were about to combust? But the fact that they were so much more sporadic and less intense only deepened my concerns about my bond with Maude. There had been a definite connection between the hot flashes and the buildup of my magical power, ever since I first found the typewriter. When my inspiration had been at its peak, they had seemed to come in waves, as strong as they were unavoidable.

And now?

Nada, besides a low-key flush every so often.

Was this permanent? I had no way of knowing. It would have been helpful to have someone to talk to, but with Patrick gone, I was left to stew in my own juices. A few times I caught myself thinking about Connie, but contacting her wasn't even a possibility right now. I truly did believe that her initial intentions were good. My jailer the other night had said as much. She's been under the spell of some other magical item that had forced her into being an operative for the Organization. Which meant that, as much as I wanted to, I couldn't trust her. But, boy, would it have been nice to talk to someone who could shed some light on what was happening to me. I felt utterly, completely lost.

I let out a long sigh and stood, realizing how stiff my muscles were. The healing wound on my stomach gave a tiny pang of protest, but Patrick was telling the truth about one thing. I was definitely healing far faster than I would have before this all started.

Speaking of Patrick...

I glanced down at my watch and my stomach clenched. He'd been gone for hours. The sun was surely coming up by now, and we couldn't even risk venturing out to look for him.

I gnawed my lip, worried—not for *him,* of course, but about the possibility that he had double-agented on me again and decided to turn us all over to the Organization. Or maybe they tracked him down while he was getting supplies and were torturing the truth out of him right this moment. Or maybe he just decided we weren't worth his time and gave up on the whole thing. Or--

I closed my eyes, telling myself to relax.

As if reading my mind, Mee-maw leaned back in her seat, letting out a yawn. "Where the heck did he get off to, anyway? We--"

But she was interrupted by a loud thumping noise above us, followed by the discernible sound of footsteps. Mee-maw opened her mouth, but I shook my head frantically.

"Shh!" Heart pounding in my chest, I made my way over to the door. Yep, the sound was definitely footsteps, and seemed to be heading our way. I glanced over my shoulder at Zoe, muttering, "Stay here and take care of Mee-maw. If I scream, go straight to the police. Do you understand?" Zoe gave a worried nod, and I slowly pushed open the door and crept out into the hall. I knew it was probably just Patrick coming back, but if it was, he was sure taking his sweet time with it. And if it wasn't? Well...

I skulked down the darkened hallway, mentally kicking myself for forgetting to grill Mee-maw about her gun and if she'd brought along bullets for it.

Leaning against the wall outside one of the other rooms was

a broom, which I grabbed in front of me like a weapon. I didn't want to turn the lights on, which meant feeling my way around the next corner, moving on tiptoes so as not to make any noise. The sound of a door closing behind me nearly made me jump out of my skin, and I whirled around, brandishing the broom. A light flicked on a moment later, blinding me, and I began to swing frantically until I heard a muffled, *"Ooph"*.

As my eyes adjusted to the light, I saw Patrick, doubled over and clutching his stomach, where I had jabbed him with the top of the broom. "What the hell, Cricket?" he groaned, staring up at me in disbelief.

I swallowed, my cheeks heating. "You'd been gone so long, we were starting to think you weren't coming back."

He gestured behind him, where there were scattered a half a dozen bags full of supplies. "I had a lot of stuff to do," he reminded me, straightening. I moved to help him retrieve his things as he continued, "Then I had to hide the car, remember? I've still got to go back and get some more bags."

"Oh." My face went even hotter. "I, uh... That makes sense." I cleared my throat. "Sorry I hit you," I added lamely. It struck me then that I *had* been worried about him, and my relief at having him back here was palpable.

Seeming to sense where my mind had gone, Patrick leaned in closer to me, meeting my eyes with his. "I need you to know something, Cricket," he said, his tone urgent. "I can't make up for what I did, but I want you to know that I'd never do that again. I'm so very sorry."

"Patrick," I began quietly, "I--"

But he put up a hand to quiet me. "I just wanted to get that off my chest. And to let you know that I'm working on fixing what's broken inside of me. My father's mind is twisted," he said. "And he twisted mine the same way. I'm trying to rectify that now, but I can't change my past. All I can do is try to be a better man in the future."

I nodded, swaying in place and leaning toward him, the pull impossible to resist. "You're already doing that," I replied, the broom falling from my hands and clattering to the floor. He looked so strong in that moment, so stable, in a sea of chaos. A breathless moment later, I felt myself rolling up on my toes, leaning in as he reached out a hand to cup my jaw.

My lips were inches from his when a gravelly voice boomed, "Hey, before you two kids head off to Bonetown, me and Zoe gotta show you something."

I jerked back with a start as Patrick straightened. It was probably a good thing Mee-maw had saved me from doing something stupid, but dang, it didn't feel like it in the moment.

"Yup, be right in," Patrick murmured, his voice husky.

Awkwardness ensued as Mee-maw scurried away and Patrick and I bent to collect the rest of the bags. Wordlessly, we brought them back to the other room to find Zoe perched in front of Greg's laptop. Her eyes were bright with excitement as she waved us over.

"You guys have to hear this," she said, getting to her feet. "Mee-maw and I were doing some more digging on crone's covens. We started with that site where she found A. Cromwell's letter about the Crow's Feet Coven, and also checked out that wiccan message board you signed up for, Gaia's Gathering. From what we've read so far, most witches in the coven had a base level of magic once they came into their power—magic over and above their special talent, I mean. And it's not just faster healing and more vitality."

A nugget of hope formed in my chest. "That would explain why I was able to uproot that tree trying to escape the other night."

But that had been when Maude and I were still tightly bound...

"What if there's an...issue with your connection to your item?" I glanced over at Maude. "Would a witch still have the ability to use other magic?"

"Supposedly, once she makes the initial, first spell with her item, it awakens the magic inside her. I don't think that goes away," Mee-maw said and then shrugged. "Well, that's what MountainGoddess79 seems to think, anyway."

Another reason the Organization would want to kill a witch after the separation ceremony. If my powers were already strong enough to uproot a freaking tree, imagine what a strong witch might do to them in retaliation for taking her item if they didn't kill her?

"Anyway, they've made a list of all sorts of basic spells, and ways of harnessing your magic," Mee-maw said.

"We figured, while we wait for you and Maude to reconnect, this would give you something to do," Zoe added.

"I mean..." I bit my lip. "I guess it's worth a shot."

"Exactly," Mee-maw crowed as she clapped her hands. "Here--" She grabbed a pencil off the table and held it up. "Try to make this float."

I eyed it dubiously. "And how do you propose I do that?" I'd done the tree thing out of desperation, not by design. Later that same night, I'd tried to take down my prison guard using magic, and that had nearly worked, too. But the circumstances were very different. Staring at the pencil with all eyes on me and no one about to murder me? I was at a loss as to how to harness the feelings that had been churning inside me to produce the spark.

"It says right here, the trick is to close your eyes and meditate while you learn to focus your magic," Zoe replied. "If you get good enough at it, then it will become like a reflex."

I sighed and picked up the pencil, placing it in my palm and thinking back to the burst of magic I had unleashed back in Finneas' prison. Letting my eyes drift closed, I did my best to clear my mind, steadying my breathing and trying not to think about how foolish I felt in the moment. After what seemed like endless minutes, a faint stirring of something bubbled in my gut as I focused, but I couldn't be sure whether it was all in my head or not...

Until Mee-maw muttered, "Well, that was a bust."

I opened my eyes and saw with a sinking feeling that the pencil hadn't moved. The interruption had shattered my concentration, and if there *had* been a twinge in the pit of my stomach that wasn't related to the need for breakfast, it had winked out in an instant. I sighed, setting the pencil back on the table.

"I don't want to burst bubbles here, but pinning our hopes on the musings of MountainGoddess79 might not be the best way to go. Maybe we need to be looking for some older sources."

"You can't give up just like that," Zoe insisted. "Here, try turning the lights off with your mind!"

I rolled my eyes and gave it the old college try, with the same results—or lack thereof. The others continued to make suggestions, from telekinetically opening the door to raising the temperature in the room, but no matter how hard I focused, I only ended up feeling more and more like a failure. Patrick watched this all quietly from the back of the room, his expression unreadable.

Eventually, they ran out of steam, and I settled into a chair, mentally exhausted and emotionally battered, while Zoe continued to peruse the forums. Mee-maw looked at me, raising her eyebrow, before her gaze settled on Patrick.

"So," she said to him, breaking the silence, "your people— and by people, I mean the bad guys you used to run with—seem to have a lot of knowledge about witches. We're coming up empty here. Is there anything you know that might help Cricket learn to use her magic?"

Patrick's face went stormy as he crossed his arms.

"Keep in mind, I don't have a whole lot of faith in what I was told anymore," he replied slowly. "Most of it was based in folklore, and the Organization was more dedicated to hunting down witches' personal items than researching the theory of magic. Whatever I knew for sure, I've already shared. I'm sorry that I can't be of any more help."

My shoulders slumped as I looked away. I hadn't broached the topic with him yet, but I'd hoped he could tell me whether my connection with Maude was truly gone and, if not, how to get it back. The realization that he had limited knowledge in this area was crushing, to say the least.

"But don't worry. I have a plan to change that soon." He got to his feet and dug through one of the bags and pulled out a black hoodie. "I'll be back. I've got to make a call and, in order to do so, I've got to get the burner phones from the car before the library opens." He donned the sweatshirt, pulling up the hood as he headed out of the room, closing the door behind him.

"What's he got planned?" Mee-maw asked.

"I don't know," I replied. "Let's just hope it's something good."

Mee-maw stood up and I watched as she went to one of the bags Patrick had brought back, rummaging for a moment before withdrawing the white board he'd bought. She began to make a list of the spells we had tried so far, crossing each one off before returning to Zoe's side to consult the list some more.

"We'll just have to keep trying until we find something that works while we try to find potions for Zoe," she said without turning to me. "We're not giving up that easy, Cricket."

"This other guy is saying you might need an altar for using spells," Zoe spoke up, squinting at the laptop screen. "He says you can use crystals and herbs for grounding, an athame for channeling your power, and--"

"And where are we supposed to get any of that stuff?" I asked.

"There has to be some kind of a store around here," Zoe responded, "even if it's in the weird part of town. Besides, I could use some of this stuff, too. There are all kinds of potions listed here, love potions, protection potions, healing potions..."

By the time the door swung open a short while later, we were all entrenched back in our fruitless labor. It wasn't until I looked up and locked eyes with someone who was decidedly *not* Patrick that panic set in.

Trudy the librarian gaped at me and raised an accusing finger.

"What in the hells bells are you three doing here?"

CHAPTER 5

W<small>HAT WERE</small> *WE* <small>DOING HERE?</small>

What was *she* doing here? It was more than an hour before opening.

Shame on me for thinking things couldn't get any worse. I really needed to learn to stop doing that.

Trudy continued to appraise us with her sharp, blue eyes, which, combined with her aquiline nose, gave her the air of a predator. One that had just cornered its prey.

While I had respected the librarian because she clearly loved her job and took pride in excelling, I wasn't overly fond of her, personally. She was way too tightly wound for my tastes. It was time to set that aside and crank the charm up to eleven, because if we didn't talk our way out of this, we were well and truly screwed.

I glanced frantically over at Mee-maw and Zoe, who were staring, open-mouthed, having seemingly lost the ability to speak.

Come on, Cricket.

"Trudy! So nice to see you again. You look amazing, by the way. Love the cardigan. Roosters are my favorite, too. What is that color called, anyway? Mustard yellow, or more of a goldenrod--?"

She ignored my yammering as her gaze scrolled over the white board. "What is all that?"

"*That*..." I moved stealthily in front of it and continued, "is, uh, we were..."

"Playing Dungeons and Dragons!" Zoe suddenly exclaimed, the words tumbling out of her mouth in a rush. Mee-maw and I turned to gape at her, but she pressed on. "We're really trying to get into the spirit of the roleplay," she said, babbling a hundred miles an hour. "I play the witch, so I was telling Cricket, here—I mean, um...Cassandra...the warrior princess...what ingredients we needed to get at the market. Our grandmother, here, is the one running the game. That's why she was writing on the white board. We have to keep everything straight, you know?"

I didn't groan out loud, but it was a close thing.

"Uh-huh," Trudy muttered, but one look at her expression told me she wasn't buying it. "What are you doing in the library basement before we open? And how on earth did you even get in here?"

I hadn't felt this put on the spot since the teacher caught me sneaking out of detention when I was thirteen.

"A water line broke back at the house," I chimed in, re-using an excuse I'd used with Ethan a few days before when I'd been convinced he was a spy. "The plumbers won't be over until later today. And we really needed a place to go in the meantime, so..."

"So you broke into the library?" Trudy shook her head, scowling. "Like I'm supposed to believe that. What are you *really* doing here?"

"I might ask you the same question, lady," Mee-maw fired back, and I shot her a warning look. Now was not the time for attitude.

"It's my job to be here!" Trudy replied with a sniff before

approaching the white board and giving us all another, searching look. "Sage? Yew? Spring water? Rose quartz?"

"I *told* you, we were roleplaying!" Zoe insisted.

"You know what?" I said, putting my hands up and edging towards the door. "We'll just get out of your hair. We can find somewhere else. It's totally fine. We'll just pack up our stuff and--"

But my eyes went wide as Trudy made a beeline for the table where Greg's laptop sat open.

"You're not packing up anything or going anywhere. If you don't tell me what you're doing here, I'll find out for myself. Then, I'll call the authorities and let them throw you in the slammer!"

"Hey! You can't--" Mee-maw began, but it was too late. The librarian was already reading the open page. I winced as I watched her eyes flit back and forth, and the tension mounted as she glanced back over her shoulder at the white board before returning her gaze to the computer screen.

I had given up hope of getting out of this easily, and had all my energy focused on willing Mee-maw to keep her gun "holstered" when Trudy let out a gasp.

"Oh my god." Her cheeks had gone bone white as she looked from me, to Mee-maw, to Zoe. Her voice dropped to almost a whisper. "You're...witches?"

"Uh..." Zoe stared at her. "No?"

Trudy shook her head. "No...Yes, you are. You absolutely are." She grabbed Greg's laptop and spun it around, displaying the several tabs of Gaia's Gathering forum posts that Zoe had opened before. "I know this website," she said in a hushed whisper, but this time it was tinged with...excitement? No, that couldn't be right. The only emotion Trudy was capable of was barely-disguised disdain. "Gaia's Gathering!" she exclaimed. "For wiccans! Is *that* what you were doing? Researching spells?"

I blinked, flabbergasted. This day was just getting weirder and weirder.

"What the heck do you know about Gaia's Gathering?" Mee-maw demanded, putting her hands on her hips.

Trudy looked over at her, her expression softening. "I happen to be a regular user of these forums and a level ninety-eight poster on Gaia's Gathering," she replied coolly. Turning back to the computer, she continued, "Studying wicca is a hobby of mine. Drat—I wish I had brought my crystals with me. Usually, I leave them out on the back porch to charge in the sun during the day. If I had known there were other practitioners here, though..." Seemingly catching herself, she straightened up and cleared her throat. "Is that why you're here? Wait, don't tell me..." She frowned, staring me down unnervingly. "It's because you're worried about the Freemason Lodge up in Longdale, isn't it? You don't want anyone around town to know what you're doing, I get it. Wow." She shook her head disbelievingly. "Now it all makes sense. And here I was thinking you were down here planning a bank robbery or something! You know we share a basement wall with American Federal next door..."

Zoe and I could only gape at the librarian, whose demeanor had seemingly changed on a dime. Who the heck was this lady, and what had she done with the stickler who told you off if you returned a book so much as a day late?

Mee-maw, however, seemed to have latched on to the bit about the Lodge. "The Freemasons?" she asked. "I have so many theories about them!" Her eyes narrowing, she took a step forward. "Do you know anything about the...*Illuminati?*"

"Oh, sure," Trudy replied gamely, ignoring my and Zoe's chorus of groans. "Did you know there are allegedly three independent Illuminati agents in this county alone? Although, some sources estimate that number might be closer to five."

"I'll be damned," Mee-maw said, running a hand through her silver hair and looking over to me and Zoe.

Trudy shuffled back around the table, her earlier suspicion having vanished in a heartbeat. Her gaze settled on the typewriter and cauldron on the other side of the room, and I felt a surge of concern as she approached the table to scrutinize our magical items. She stopped in front of the cauldron, placing a hand gently on its metal surface and closing her eyes.

"Sweet. I can feel the magic coming off of this," she said after a moment, turning back to look at us. "Is this made of pewter, or iron?"

"Uh..." Zoe flushed a little. "I'm not sure. I'm actually kind of new to this, uh...witch stuff. Like, *really* new. We all are."

"I guess it's a good thing I showed up when I did," Trudy said with a sage nod. "You know, you really shouldn't get into witchcraft if you haven't done your full research beforehand. It took me years just to master palmistry, and I'm still not up for practicing it on other people, yet. I just don't want to mess with fate and all."

Mee-maw nodded in agreement. "I hear that. You know, Trudy, you might just be the exact person we need. Tell me more about this Freemason Lodge."

Zoe and I watched in wonder as the two older women began to talk conspiracy theories, peppering each other with questions and speculations as if they had known each other their whole lives. My heart rate was only just beginning to return to normal, and Zoe seemed as taken aback as I was. Speaking of fate, this was one hell of a twist of the stuff, and that wasn't lost on either of us—what were the odds that the librarian who walked in on us would turn out to be interested in magic?

My mind drifted back to my first meeting with Patrick, a seemingly random encounter that had turned out to be too good to be true. Then again, though, this was Rocky Knoll, and if one thing had become clear to me recently, it was that the town hosted far more occult activities than it appeared to. There was also the issue of the Organization— would they really recruit a practicing wiccan as a way of tracking us down? They didn't even know we were hiding out here, unless Patrick had told them...which I found myself doubting, for better or worse.

Bringing anyone else into the fold at this point was a huge gamble. But, given what she'd already seen, I was sensing we had little choice. She might know something about magical abilities and how to use them but, more importantly, maybe we could convince her to let us stay hidden down here. Hell, she might even be able to help us keep other prying eyes away from our hiding place.

Zoe and I exchanged a look, and she gave me a small nod; we were on the same page.

"Trudy," I said slowly. The librarian quieted immediately, meeting my eyes. "I think my grandmother is right. We could use your help."

"But we're in a bit of a sticky situation," Zoe added. "I'm not saying it's *dangerous,* per se, but--"

"It's dangerous," I interrupted her flatly, crossing my arms.

"Oh?" Trudy asked, her blue eyes filling with excitement. "Spell gone awry? Bad premonition?" Her voice dropped to an ominous whisper as fear filled her voice. "A curse?"

If she *was* acting, she'd be in line for an Oscar.

"Not exactly," I replied, letting out a long sigh. It was now or never. "The truth is, we think we *are* witches. Not just wiccans, but real, honest-to-goodness witches. But we still have no idea how our powers even work. All we know is that there's a group of witch hunters after us, and it's no longer safe to stay at our house."

I'd kept it super vague, but the whole spiel still sounded

absurd, even to my ears, and I was half-expecting Trudy to burst out laughing. Instead, she gave a somber nod.

"Some people say the old witch trials never really ended," she said in a low voice. "Rocky Knoll has a history of magical practitioners, though...and a history of violence towards them."

Apparently, convincing a person who *wanted* something to be true was pretty easy. Who knew?

"So you've heard about...the Organization?" Mee-maw asked.

"I've heard of plenty of organizations, none of them good," Trudy replied. "But if there's one thing my research has told me, it's that some cowans—non-magical folk—will fight tooth and nail to see witches wiped off the face of the earth." Her eyes met mine, and there was sympathy in her expression. "I don't know how much help I can offer you folks, but I'm willing to do what I can for you. We believers need to stick together, right?" There was a pause as she licked her lips. "Besides," she added, a little bashfully, "I've never met *real* witches before." There was a touch of reverence in her voice that I never would have expected from someone like Trudy.

At that moment, the door opened, and Patrick strode into the room.

"Sorry," he said, "I had to walk back to the car and get the bag with the burner phones in it, and--" He broke off in surprise the moment he saw Trudy.

The librarian's eyes widened. "Patrick? You're part of this all?" She drew back and gasped. "A *warlock*! This whole time I've been having you hammer nails and fix stucco and you're a warlock?"

"Uh..." Patrick shot me a baffled look.

"No," I explained. "He's helping us, although, it's a bit of a long story." I turned to him. "Trudy, here, is an occult enthusiast," I said carefully. "She's going to help us, if she can." I gave him a little shrug and a look that said, *What can you do?*

"I see," Patrick replied in a clipped tone. "Well, unfortunately, I only have the four burner phones, but--"

"That's fine," Trudy said, flapping her hand at him. "I don't need one. I've got three stashed at home, unopened, just in case. Just give me your burner numbers and I'll send you mine."

Mee-maw looked suitably impressed as Patrick doled out the burner phones, allowing us to exchange numbers with Trudy. The whole thing felt a little surreal, although that was about par for the course, at this point.

"So," Trudy said, "what do you need from me first?"

Zoe gestured at the white board. "I'd like to try brewing some potions in my cauldron. These ingredients were all suggested on the forums, but we have no idea where to find any of them."

"Leave that to me," said Trudy with a firm nod. "I know a few psychic shops downtown that should do the trick. I'll text you my number, you can send me the ingredients, and I'll pick them up after my shift." She glanced down at her watch with a start. "Speaking of which, I'd better go. The library opens in thirty minutes and I've got to prep. But don't worry," she added as she reached the door, "I'll be back later."

With that, she swept out of the room like a tornado, leaving us to face a gobsmacked-looking Patrick.

"What in the hell was that?"

I cleared my throat and shrugged defensively. "Look, we didn't have much of a choice, okay? She caught us talking about witchcraft red-handed. Our options were to let Mee-maw off her with her revolver or let her in on at least the basics. We're just lucky she seems to be in our corner."

I hadn't told Patrick about my last prediction with Maude —*Trust only three*—but it was buzzing like a nest of hornets in my mind now. Back then, I'd only had to wonder if that meant I should trust Patrick or Ethan. Now, I was really pressing my luck. But Trudy strolling in on us had left us precious few options. She had been about to call the police, which would've alerted our enemies to our presence and all but served me and Maude up to them on a platter. Prediction or no, I felt like we needed Trudy on our side, at least in the short-term. I just had to hope that my gut was right on this one.

I watched silently as Patrick paced in circles for a few long moments and then finally let out a sigh.

"All right. Well, there's nothing to be done about it now. She might end up being useful. Especially now." He met and held my gaze. "I made a phone call back at the car—to a friend. She's been sort of distancing herself from the Organization since she had her daughter, saying she needed a longer period of maternity leave, but I had a feeling she'd been having some doubts. On a hunch, I reached out. She was afraid to say much, with a family to protect, but she did tell me she was trying to find a way out from under the Organization's thumb and did give me one good tidbit."

"Well?" Mee-maw demanded. "What is it? Don't keep us in suspense."

"Apparently, active Organization members from all around the world are currently in New York for some kind of conference," Patrick replied. "A conference to deal with the crone's coven that's emerging in Rocky Knoll. Looks like they're ready to bring out the big guns after you escaped, Cricket."

My heart leapt to my throat. "You mean...they're calling an international meeting just to deal with *us*?"

Patrick nodded. "That's how I felt, at first. But then I was thinking it could actually work in our favor."

"How?" asked Zoe, incredulously.

"The meeting is happening tomorrow in New York City,"

Patrick answered. "And it's an all-hands meeting, which means anyone in the know will be present. It's likely that the higher-ups are already there and the rest of the operatives are en route. That means only a couple lackeys will be left here to see if we come back to Rocky Knoll. If I had to guess, I'd say they'll be patrolling Connie's shop, Mee-maw's, the bakery, and Zoe's house...But I think that's something we can handle. It's too risky to take direct action tonight because if they spot us, it might give them time to send some of their forces back here, but tomorrow will be a perfect opportunity to get what we need, as far as additional supplies."

"Well," I began, "we don't really need much mo--"

"Cricket," Patrick cut in smoothly, shooting a glance toward Mee-maw before meeting my gaze again. "We all need to keep our strength up and, to do so, we all need to make sure we're getting quality sleep. We've got to get some futon mats or something in here, not to mention some weapons to defend ourselves in case we're discovered before you and Zoe work out how to use your magic effectively."

Zoe let out a groan of relief. "Oh, thank God." We all turned to stare at her questioningly, and she sighed, running a hand through her hair. "Look, I didn't want to say anything, at first, because I didn't think it was worth mentioning," she explained, breaking eye contact with me. "I don't know if I can really even explain it. It's just that I've had this...*feeling*, ever since we got to Greg's—sort of an itchy feeling, you know? Like there's stuff I need at the bakery, but I don't know what." She shook her head. "That sounds insane, but it's true."

I knew the feeling.

"It might not be insane," I suggested. "Maybe being there with all those ingredients might help you with your potion making."

She twisted her hands together. And shrugged. "I hate to be

that guy, but I feel like it would. That's where I'm in my element. Plus, I'd have a heat source, too. Oh!" She snapped her fingers and turned to face me. "And remember, I have a daybed in my office there!"

She did, indeed, and we'd both used it many times on those days when she had so many orders, one or both of us had to go in at two AM to pop a tray in and would take a cat nap in between batches.

"Between that and the removable cushions on the benches in the shop, I wonder if we should consider moving there for good," Zoe continued. "We'll definitely be more comfortable there. Plus, it's really close to the police station, which might be a deterrent for people with a hankering to kidnap and murder us."

All true.

But the bakery was on a main road, and despite the various rooms not visible from the street, it didn't feel quite as clandestine and hidden as the library basement. Then again, if Zoe needed to be there to manifest her powers, anyway...

I was squarely on the fence. But all it took was a glance at Mee-maw's weary face and pale skin to tip me over the edge. No matter how much of a spitfire she was, at her age and with her health issues, she needed hot meals and a comfortable place to sleep, at the very least.

It was a no brainer.

"I vote we give it a try. We pack up, go and at least see if being there helps Zoe with her powers. If not, or we feel like we're too exposed, we reevaluate. "

Mee-maw nodded. "Yup. If most of the Organization is going to be out of town anyway, then I say we might as well."

Patrick put his hands in his pockets. "That seals it."

"We'll go to the bakery first thing tomorrow morning, then," I said with a nod.

"And if the place is guarded?" Zoe protested.

"They don't even know we're back in Rocky Knoll yet, and they won't have the manpower to have a guard at every possible location. My guess is they'll be mostly focused on your grandmother's house, and Connie's shop to see if we go there for help." Patrick's face became a cryptic mask. "If I'm wrong and there's a guard, I'll take care of it."

I rounded on him. "I don't want anyone killed if we can help it, Patrick. Not even Organization members. I don't want blood on my hands, and I'm pretty sure I'm speaking for Zoe and Mee-maw when I say that, too." I stole a glance at Mee-maw, who was leaning on the table, looking as gung-ho as ever. "Well, I'm pretty sure I'm speaking for Zoe, at least," I amended.

"We won't need to resort to violence," Patrick told me, putting a hand on my shoulder. I didn't shrug it off. "I'm pretty good at getting what I want."

At that moment, his phone began to ring. Stealing a glance at it, he gave me an apologetic look before putting it up to his ear and excusing himself.

I stared after him, unsure what to think. Yeah, so maybe he wasn't a bad guy anymore, but there was more to find out about Patrick Byrne.

He had secrets.

And I was going to find out what they were.

CHAPTER 6

C*OME ON*, *old girl,* I thought, *give me something.* But Maude just continued to stare up at me accusingly, the same as the night before.

I tipped back in my chair and stretched my neck, wincing when it gave out an audible pop. I had been sitting here for going on an hour, trying desperately to summon my magic, to feel that familiar spark again, but so far...nothing.

Not a single word.

On top of the strange sense of loss and grief at the lack of connection between Maude and I, there was also the sense of responsibility weighing on my chest like an anvil. How was I supposed to help get us out of this mess if I couldn't even use any of my powers?

The new day had started out so well, too. After a relatively smooth morning, I'd been holding out hope that things were finally on the upswing for us again. We had gotten an early start, as planned, so that we could pack up our things and head to the bakery. We were all feeling on edge, and none of us had slept very well the night before. Trying to get some rest in those dusty old chairs had left us all cranky and sore, with Mee-maw looking particularly worse for wear for the first couple hours—our basement slumber party hadn't done any favors for her sciatica.

But for all that, getting to the bakery—something I had been nervous about ever since it had been brought up—had gone off without a hitch. In the early morning light, the streets had been largely empty. Patrick had gone to fetch the car and had taken a ride by the bakery before picking us up. He seemed more than pleased to report that there was no one guarding it. With no idea how long that window would be open, we'd packed up the car and hustled over.

It had all worked out...well, rather perfectly, but I guess it was my own fault for getting too optimistic. We were still in the thick of it, as Maude's resistance was proving to me now.

Well, maybe all hope wasn't lost. Trudy had come to us in the basement before we'd left, her arms full of bags; she had gone out and gotten us as many of the supplies we had texted her as she could find. Everything from potion ingredients and ritual components, to alleged tools for casting spells she had thought might come in handy, and snacks. More than that, though, she had brought us some interesting information about the town's witch population—nothing that could help us against the Organization, but she was already proving to be a valuable set of eyes and ears.

The librarian had seemed positively crestfallen that we were leaving so soon, and I had to admit to feeling a little bad for leaving. Her excitement about having met real witches had been almost childlike.

We had told Trudy that leaving might end up being temporary, and ended up asking her for another favor, which she had happily obliged. Her assignment was now to research as much about the town's witchy history as she could—more specifically, the history of the tiny old cemetery on the outskirts of town. Back before we were being hunted by the Organization, still unaware of just how deep the conspiracy went—a time that by now felt like years ago, even though it was really only a matter of days—Mee-maw had shown us a photograph taken of the cemetery back in the early 1900s. The graves had been old, all dating back to the beginning of the 19th century, but the dates hadn't been as interesting as the fact that many of them had been removed from the plot sometime before 1984.

A coincidence? Maybe. But if this set of escalating misadventures had taught me anything, it was that there wasn't such a thing as a coincidence around Rocky Knoll. Someone would have wanted those gravestones removed, someone with the resources to get rid of them—and something to hide. Trudy had been gung ho to help us so far—maybe a little *too* gung ho, truth be told—and although I felt a little bad asking her for all these favors, we weren't exactly in the position to be turning our noses up at help. In the end, she had seemed a happy camper to have a task, and had gone as far as to wish us *"Godspeed!"* as we left, with the promise to check in on us via burner phone as soon as she found anything out.

All in all, things seemed to be working in our favor.

With the exception of any magic.

I was now perched behind a table in the back of the bakery, the noxious smells wafting over to me from the kitchen not doing anything to help me keep my focus. *If she doesn't give us all gas poisoning, I'll consider this a win,* I thought rather uncharitably, before letting out a long sigh.

I ran a hand through my hair and stood up, pushing the chair in and letting my head drop between my shoulders as I leaned on it. I felt older than I had in a long time, and although I wanted to chalk that up to a lack of good sleep, I wasn't so sure.

In spite of all these wheels that were now in motion, we still had very little in the way of payoff, aside from a more comfortable place for Mee-maw to rest. Zoe was left to try learning how to use her cauldron with only directions from the internet, and I was stewing in my own juices while Mee-maw squeezed a nap in. Patrick had taken a quick walk around to make sure that any view inside the shop from the street was obscured. Then, he'd slipped off to procure some weapons and call his contact for more information about the Organization meeting, which meant the three of us were stuck here in limbo. Trying, failing, trying, failing on a constant loop.

It was hella-demoralizing.

The sound of footsteps had me straightening up and turning around, only to see Zoe on the approach, brandishing a wooden spoon. There was something positively ungodly stuck to the end of it, and I did my best not to look at it, already knowing what was coming.

"Open up." She held the spoon out for me like a parent trying to feed an unruly infant.

I groaned. "Zoe..."

"Come on, please." She waved the spoon in my face. "I think I'm getting close this time, I swear."

"You're not going to be happy until you poison me!"

"Well, practice makes perfect, right?" Zoe grinned. "Here comes the choo-choo, chugga chugga..."

I sighed, plugged my nose, and opened my mouth, not wanting to think about whatever it was that Zoe had been working on in there. Better to just choke it down and hope for the best. It tasted like tar, and it was only through sheer force of will that I was able to swallow it without gagging, a shiver going through me as I tried desperately to purge the taste from my mouth.

"Well?" Zoe asked, crossing her arms. "Feel anything?"

"Other than disgust? No?" I held my hands out. "What am I supposed to be feeling?"

Zoe sighed, rubbing the back of her neck. "It's supposed to be a glamour spell," she replied, "although, I have to say, you're not looking very enchanted." Her shoulders sagged. "I've been at this for hours, and nothing's working. That one is supposed to be the simplest one, too."

I wanted to reassure her, but had zero ammunition for the task. She had spent the whole day making foul-smelling potions using weird combinations of ingredients, each one tasting worse than the last and with no tangible effects. It seemed I wasn't the only one who was lacking witchy inspiration.

"Look," I said, hoping to come across as more optimistic than I felt, "you're probably just not in the right mindset, you know? I know that when I wrote on Maude I always had to be 'in the zone'. I tried forcing it, and it never worked." I cast a guilty glance over my shoulder at the typewriter. "It's *still* not working."

I watched my cousin slump into a nearby chair, pulling a face. I could tell she was getting frustrated, the same way I was, and the sensible voice in my mind that was suggesting I give it a rest and come back to it later was only making me all the more irritated.

"I suck at this," Zoe muttered, staring down at the wooden spoon. She lifted it cautiously to her nose, gave it a tentative sniff, and grimaced. "Jeez, that smells like used motor oil."

She was spot on, but there was no point in saying so. After a few silent moments, she stood with a sigh.

"Back to the drawing board."

Afternoon wore into evening, the sky slowly changing color as we continued our fruitless efforts. I was glad to see Mee-maw still napping; getting her to lie down had been like pulling teeth, but she needed it. As much of a toll as this was all taking on my cousin and me, it was that much worse for our old grandmother, and we were going to need to be as close to a hundred percent as possible if we were going to come out the other end.

It wasn't until the smells drifting from the kitchen suddenly stopped being noxious that I pulled my attention away from the typewriter.

Call me crazy, I thought, sitting up in my chair, *but that smells like...*

Cinnamon buns. Zoe's specialty. She must have finally thrown in the towel, and I couldn't blame her. The smell called to me like a siren's song, and I stood up and followed it into the kitchen, where Zoe was leaning against the counter, a grim smile tipping her lips.

"Hey," she said, not looking up.

"Hey," I echoed, crossing my arms. "Still no luck?"

"Zilch." She shook her head sadly. "I figured I'd do something I know I'm good at. Sweets make everything better, right?"

"You're gosh-diddly-darn right, they do," came Mee-maw's voice, and we turned to see her standing in the doorway, her eyes bleary and her slate gray mullet tousled. "Are those your cinnamon rolls, Zoe?"

"They sure are," Zoe replied, moving to check on them. Pulling open the oven only made the smell stronger, and I couldn't help but cheer up a little. "And I put the kettle on."

"Well, count me in," Mee-maw said, grinning.

A few minutes later, we were all seated around the table, a cinnamon roll and a mug of tea in front of each of us. I felt slightly revitalized by the normalcy of it all, almost enough to forget about my struggles with Maude for a moment.

Almost.

"How was your nap, Mee-maw?" Zoe asked through a mouthful of sticky confection.

"It wasn't a nap. I was just having a good, long thing. Don't coddle me. I'm fine," Mee-maw shot back. "Besides, when I nap, I wind up staying awake until all hours."

"Well, wouldn't that just be the same as every night, Mee-maw?" I asked her, taking a sip of tea. "Don't act like you're not up all night researching the Denver airport conspiracy, or whatever the heck else it is you get up to on those crazy sites you go on."

"Those *crazy sites* of mine," Mee-maw replied, "are going to be what gets us through all this. Just you wait. Forget this magical artifact mumbo-jumbo. I'm older than both of you, and I'm going to save us with the power of technology."

I laughed. "Whatever you say, Mee-maw."

"That's the right answer, kiddo." She glanced down at her empty plate in surprise, licking a drop of frosting off her finger. "You know what? I want another one of these. Forget the sciatica. I feel like a million bucks."

"Go for it," Zoe replied with a chuckle. "They're on the counter."

Mee-maw sprang to her feet, but as she did, her elbow shot out and nicked the handle of her teacup. A second later, it was airborne.

I reached out for it in vain as it went careening towards the linoleum floor, only to remain suspended in midair, trembling slightly as if fighting its own battle with gravity.

My eyes went wide, and I stared at my hand in shock. A second later, the cup fell the rest of the way to the ground, shattering and splashing our legs with tepid tea, but we hardly even noticed.

The others were both staring at me like...well, like I'd just done a magic trick.

Zoe clapped her hands together in glee. "You're back, baby! You're back!"

CHAPTER 7

I STARED down at the porcelain fragments on the floor, the sound of my heartbeat loud in my ears. Slowly, I looked up, turning from Zoe to Mee-maw. Their eyes were as big as dinner plates.

"That totally happened, right?" I asked. "I mean, I didn't just imagine that, did I?"

"Unless we're all just imagining levitating teacups now, then no," Zoe replied. "It was floating for a second, there." She met my eyes. "How'd you do it?"

"I have no idea." I shook my head, tunneling a hand through my hair. "It just happened. I wasn't even thinking about it. It was like, instinct or something. Crazy," I breathed, staring down at my hands. A surge of triumph washed over me. The hows or whys didn't seem to matter at the moment as much as the fact that I had actually done it...and they had witnessed it this time.

"Well, don't just sit there," Zoe exclaimed. "Do it again!"

"Yeah," Mee-maw agreed, pointing at the teapot on the counter. "Do that one next!"

"Guys--" I began, but I couldn't finish the sentence. A hot flash, as fast as a bullet train and as intense as a high fever, crashed down on me out of nowhere, nearly knocking me off balance as I stared down at the remains of the teacup. My body felt like I'd swallowed a nuclear reactor, and my fingers were throbbing as if someone had just taken a hammer to my hands. The energy was overwhelming, and I sprang to my feet before I was even aware of what I was doing.

"Cricket?" Zoe asked, furrowing her brow. "Are you all right?"

I scurried out of the kitchen, all thoughts of potion brewing, cinnamon rolls, and floating teacups gone from my mind. There was only one thing that mattered right now, and I felt like if I didn't get to it, I was going to explode. Making a beeline for the table in the connecting room, I rushed to where I'd put Maude. She was still there, exactly as I had left her, but the old machine suddenly felt full of life and promise as I dropped into the chair and stared it down. I realized that I was trembling, although whether from relief or anticipation, I couldn't say, and it felt like my hands were moving of their own accord as they settled on the old keys, poised to channel whatever it was that was now rushing through me. I could feel my eyes going out of focus, my mind taking on a fuzzy haziness, followed by a bright burst of inspiration, an idea so clear and powerful that it cut through all other thought completely.

I could hear the others murmuring to one another as they followed me to the table, but I wasn't paying attention to what they were saying as my fingers began to move, racing over the keys as if possessed. A prediction. The old spark. Back, and just as intense as ever. The sentence burst out of me, and only then was I able to bring myself back to the present moment, the trance lifting slightly as I became aware of Mee-maw and Zoe standing behind me, staring at Maude over my shoulders. The hot flash seemed to abate a little now that the words were out, my senses coming back to me a little, and in unison, the three of us looked down at the words I had typed on the page.

Evil thrives in the cover of darkness. Turn on the kitchen light, and the cockroaches will scatter.

"What does that mean?" Zoe asked, putting a hand on my shoulder and turning to look at me.

"I have no idea," I replied, shaking my head, still shaking from the rush of adrenaline. "It just came out. I guess it's back," I said, hardly daring to even believe the words.

"Yay!" Zoe beamed. "So now we just need to figure out what it means, right?"

"Yeah," I began, but before I knew what was happening, the hot flash was on me again, just as strong and insistent as the last time. My skin was prickling with magic, the hairs on the back of my neck standing up as an electric current coursed through me. I reached out and tore the sheet from the typewriter, setting it aside before winding a new page in, my hands shaking. The others' excited commentary died down when they realized I wasn't done, and I once again let the magic take the wheel as another prediction began to pour out of me.

The future is ever changing.

You nearly paid the ultimate price by disregarding the warning and trusting too many. Alas, now more threat lies in trusting too few.

There is safety in numbers. Remember, a rabbit hides, but a pack of wolves walks freely.

Step into your power.

I could feel the feverishness subsiding once again, although, this time, it seemed to be receding entirely, leaving me to frown as I went over the typed words again and again, trying and failing to make sense of them. This one was longer, but equally cryptic. For a few moments, none of us spoke, and I leaned back in my chair, pursing my lips.

"Well, what on earth does that mean?" Mee-maw demanded, throwing her hands up in frustration. "And why are these so frigging vague? What happened to the first few predictions that were super long and clear?" She put a hand on the table, leaning a broad hip against it. "They used to be different. You'd write, 'a giraffe is going to break out of a zoo'. Boom, a giraffe breaks out of the zoo. What is this cloak and dagger fortune cookie malarkey?"

"Right?" Zoe said. "Before the ritual, they were a lot more literal. They spelled out exactly what was going to happen. These are different." She pressed her lips together. "Are you sure it was the same kind of magic, Cricket?"

"I mean, I think so," I replied, rubbing a hand over my forehead. "It felt the same. There was the hot flash, the surge of inspiration, the feeling like I wasn't really the one writing it...It was all there."

"Do you think maybe that's it, then?" Zoe asked. "Maybe the ritual affected the predictions somehow, even though they didn't get to finish it?"

"I guess that's possible."

Mee-maw was silent, her lips pursed as she read and reread the words on the paper. There was a fresh gleam in her eye, color in her cheeks, and she looked more energized than she had in a long time. The nap must have done her a world of good.

"I don't think it's that," she said, turning to look at us. "Bear with me, here. The earlier predictions were really specific, right? Like the one about my heart, or the shark attack. Those were all for events that were just about to happen. What if these new predictions are more vague because they're talking about things farther in the future?"

"So, imminent events are more clear?" I asked.

She shrugged her shoulders. "It's a thought."

"That would make sense," Zoe added, pointing at the first

line of the new prediction. "It says here, 'the future is ever changing'. We know that's true, because you saved Mee-maw and that changed your prediction, remember?"

"Makes sense," I agreed, my voice thoughtful.

"On the other hand, your magic may have just taken a wonky turn since the run-in with the Organization," Mee-maw put in. "It could be anything. We're not exactly experts, here. I can put out some feelers online, see if anyone has any ideas."

"Be careful and cryptic about posting," Zoe warned her. "Reading is one thing, but the Organization could be watching the forums. We can't tip them off about any of this."

"Well, I was going to spell out our exact names and location, maybe an invitation just for good measure, but now that you mention it, Zoe..."

I watched as my cousin backed away from the table, crossing her arms as she began to pace. At first, I wasn't sure if my eyes were playing tricks on me, but then I looked closer.

Yup.

Something was definitely different.

It was subtle, but still noticeable: her hair seemed longer, more lustrous, somehow. There was a glow about her, a sort of unmistakable youthfulness. And something else, too...

"Zoe," I said, interrupting her and Mee-maw's bickering, "is it just me, or have you lost weight?"

"Have I...?" She frowned, glancing down at herself. "I don't think so. Why?"

"You look thinner. And your hair looks nice."

"I'll be darned," Mee-maw observed. "She's right, Zoe."

I watched as my cousin crossed the room to where a full-length mirror hung on the opposite wall. She scrutinized her reflection, turning around slowly before leaning in to examine her face.

"Wowza! You're not kidding!" she exclaimed suddenly,

whirling back around and gesturing at her temple. "And that age spot by my hairline is gone—the one I hated! How on earth...?"

"You know," Mee-maw cut in as she stood and rolled her shoulders back. "Now that you mention it, I feel a lot better, too. My sciatica hasn't been this good since...Well, ever, actually. Man, I feel like I could run a marathon!" She gave me a gleeful grin. "You sure you didn't write a story about giving us back our youth, Cricket?"

I cast around fruitlessly for some connection and then stilled. "Guys, hold on—we've all improved somehow." I stood up, ticking things off on my fingers. "Zoe, you look better. Mee-maw, your sciatica is gone and you feel energized, and me? Well, I was finally able to write on Maude again..." I turned to my cousin. "Could it have been one of your potions, Zoe?"

She shook her head. "I don't think so. We all tasted different ones. Maybe it was the chamomile tea?"

Mee-maw snorted. "Chamomile tea is for old ladies. I didn't drink a sip of that crap."

Zoe's eyes went wide. "The cinnamon rolls! I was trying to do a wish fulfillment potion before I made them. Sort of a 'heart's desire' thing. I screwed it up, and was at my breaking point mentally, and figured you were, too. I wanted to make the cinnamon buns to cheer everyone up. Although, now that I think about it, I don't really even remember what I put in them and didn't even realize I'd cooked the caramel sauce in the cauldron. I wasn't even thinking about it, I just sort of did it. Like I was on autopilot. Almost in a..."

"Trance. Like when I write on Maude," I finished for her. "You must have found a way to make the spell work through baking, Zoe. And it gave us each what we wanted most in that moment."

"Hot dog!" Mee-maw exclaimed, before turning to give Zoe an incredulous look. "Wait. Pump the brakes a second. You're telling me *that's* what you wanted most right now?" Her tone went shrill. "Better hair and a smaller tuckus?"

"No! Of course not. It was just a passing thought!" Zoe protested, cheeks going pink. "I had glanced in the mirror when I went to wash my hands and was thinking...doesn't matter. What I really wanted was to succeed at making one of these potions work." Her face lit up with a smile. "And I did it. The rest was just a bonus, I guess."

"Do you have any idea what you put into the cauldron that deviated from your usual recipe?"

A shadow passed over Zoe's face and she frowned. "Actually, I don't. Not a clue," she replied. "Like I said, it was practically like I was in a trance."

"So what are we waiting for, then?" Mee-maw asked, already heading back toward the kitchen. "There's plenty more where that came from, and I could stand a little less gray in my hair."

"Nuh, uh-uh," Zoe said, catching her arm and stopping her. "We can't just eat them all now! We have to save them for emergencies."

"Zoe's right," I agreed, coming to stand beside them. "Especially if she might not be able to recreate the recipe."

"You and your logic," Mee-maw said, sighing. "But I guess you're right. Let's get them wrapped up and put them somewhere safe, then."

Together, we made short work of the cleanup, putting the cinnamon buns in the refrigerator and cleaning up the broken teacup. A few minutes later, we were back around the kitchen table, trying to puzzle out the meaning of my most recent predictions.

"It says to turn on the kitchen light," Zoe was saying, glancing at the typewritten prediction. "Like, shining a light on the whole thing? The Organization, the conspiracies, all of it?"

"Maybe," Mee-maw said, nodding. "Could also mean to walk around in the open, you know? And sticking together. No splitting up like those Scooby-Doo kids. That's when they run into real trouble."

"The other one is what's bothering me," I admitted. "The one from before said to 'trust only three', but now it's talking about a pack of wolves and safety in numbers. Which is it?"

"This one, if I had to guess," Zoe replied. "It's more recent, after all. And the future is ever-changing, remember?"

"So maybe we were right to trust Patrick and Trudy," I said, crossing my arms. It would be a lie to say that didn't make me feel a little better, especially as far as Patrick was concerned; if trust was now the operative word, then maybe giving him a second chance wasn't a mistake after all.

"Hey, I'm all for less sneaking around," Zoe said, crossing her arms. "If this means we can afford to be a little more confident, then..." She shrugged. "I'm not complaining."

"I think I'm going to go write down what I remember of all the predictions you've made so far, Cricket," Mee-maw said, her voice turning businesslike. "I'm itching to do something. Maybe this will help us figure out if there's a pattern. There could be some rules to it that we don't understand yet."

"Sounds like a plan," Zoe agreed. "I think I might try another potion. I'm kind of feeling some muffins with a lemon glaze. Actually, I need some more sugar from the cellar."

"Go get started," I told her. "I'll go down and grab it for you."

"Thanks," Zoe said, already turning back to the cabinet and pulling out the cauldron. Mee-maw disappeared into the other room, leaving me to tromp down into the basement where Zoe kept all the bulk ingredients for the bakery. It was dimly-lit down there, but I was so invigorated by what had happened that the dark didn't bother me.

It was only as I was reaching for some sugar that I became aware of a presence beside me, and moments later, a cold hand was darting out of the darkness and grabbing hold of my arm. I nearly jumped out of my skin, sucking in a breath, and what I saw when I turned to look was nearly enough to make me fall over in shock.

Connie was staring at me out of the darkness, looking as white as a ghost, her fingers like ice as they locked around my wrist.

I let out a choked scream, the bag of sugar falling to the floor.

CHAPTER 8

CONNIE BAGSHAW. The woman who started all this. The vibrant, mysterious woman who had first connected me with Maude, setting into motion the chain of events that led me to where I was now standing.

Her eyes were flashing in the darkness of the cellar, and her crimson hair was as unkempt and wild as it had been the last time I had seen her—which, incidentally, happened to be the time she was chasing me through her shop, screaming like a banshee all the while.

Needless to say, I was frightened, adrenaline rushing through me even as my scream died in my lungs, puttering off to a croak as the shock of seeing her hit me head-on.

Is this Good Connie or Bad Connie?

I wondered feverishly, still fighting the urge to wrench my arm free of her grip. But even as I stared her down in the shadows of the basement, I could feel my anxiety fading. I peered at her more closely as my heartbeat started to settle down, a sense of inexplicable relief washing over me. Already, I could feel her touch growing warm, and something passed through us in the silence, like a burst of warmth from her hand to mine. Like a magical squeeze of reassurance.

My shoulders dropped, her warm eyes met mine, and I knew in an instant that I was looking at the real Connie. Whether she would stay that way—and for how long—was another question.

"Connie," I said, searching her face for answers. "What are you...?"

"You have nothing to fear, Cricket," Connie replied, giving my wrist a gentle squeeze before lifting our joined hands up between us. "For now. But we don't have much time."

I had been so caught up in escaping the Organization, in protecting Zoe and Mee-maw, that I had pushed my concern for the older woman to the back of my mind, but seeing her again—and not possessed by magic this time—lifted a burden I wasn't even aware I was carrying.

"I'm so glad you're safe. And the others?"

"Upstairs."

"Take me to them. I need to speak with you all."

I was bursting with questions, but I held my tongue and gave her a curt nod. Wordlessly, I led her back up the stairs, pausing on the landing at the sound of a familiar male voice; Patrick was in the kitchen, talking to Zoe, and fresh concern filled me. I hadn't been expecting him back so soon. Squaring my shoulders, I led Connie into the kitchen, pausing in the doorway to clear my throat.

Patrick and Zoe turned to me at the same time. "Zoe, I was just filling in Patrick about the good n--" My cousin's eyes widened when she saw Connie standing next to me. "Geez," she gasped, lunging for a rolling pin and holding it in front of her like a sword, "what is she doing here, Cricket?"

I held up a hand. "It's okay. She's back to normal. For now, at least." I glanced over my shoulder at the older woman, who gave me a grim nod, before continuing. "She snuck in through the basement—she needs to talk to us."

"Are you sure about this?" Patrick, who must've returned in the interim, had stood up from the table, crossing his arms as he studied Connie.

She returned his look with a solemn one of her own. "You know as well as I do that neither of us deserve their trust. But ask for it, we must." She turned to face me again. "We need to act fast."

"It's fine," I assured Patrick. "Call it a witch's intuition." The Scotsman nodded stiffly, but said nothing more.

"Where's your grandmother?" Connie asked, peering around.

"Mee-maw?" I called, beckoning to the others as we made our way out of the kitchen and into the back room, where Maude was still waiting on the table.

"Here, here," came Mee-maw's grumbling voice as she emerged from the bathroom. "Can't give a lady a minute to--" She stopped dead in her tracks when she saw Connie. "What's going on?"

"I'm here to warn you. I--" Connie's mouth snapped shut suddenly, her jaw clenching and unclenching. She took a breath and started again, "You need to understand that--" She broke off again on a choking gasp, before letting out a low growl. "Damn it...I can't..." It was obvious something was weighing on her, something she was trying to put into words.

Mee-maw raised an eyebrow, still fixing Connie with an incredulous stare as the woman looked from one of us to the next, wringing her hands helplessly.

"What's the problem? Just spit it out, toots," Mee-maw urged.

"I wasn't...myself. And now...I still..." Again, the words came out choked and stunted, and I could see the muscles in her throat working, as if she was desperately trying to make herself speak. Her mouth opened and closed again, and she let out a frustrated groan, her hand going to her neck.

"Connie?" I asked, reaching out for her. "Are you okay?"

"I'm...fine." But she shook her head vigorously even as she said it, and alarm bells started to go off in the back of my head.

"Uh oh. She's not going all Mr. Hyde again, is she?" Meemaw asked.

"Connie," I asked in a low voice, remembering what the guard who had imprisoned me had said. "Are there things you're still not allowed to say, even now, while you're not under their control?"

"Oh my gosh, that's it," Zoe said with a gasp. "She's tongue-tied. I've seen the spells for it in our research."

Connie didn't reply but the truth was etched on her face and a chill rolled through me.

The Organization had not only possessed Connie's body to use her as a spy at will, they had also made sure she couldn't tell anyone about it. I knew they had magical items in their possession—memories of that torture necklace threatened to drag me under, even now—but the scope of their power was becoming more evident, and it was frightening.

Out of the corner of my eye, I could see Patrick stiffening as he moved to the other side of the room. His arms crossed, he watched the old woman like she might burst into flames at any minute.

Spluttering and clearing her throat, she took a shaky breath in before saying, "I can't speak on certain things, but ask me questions...and if I can help, I will."

Zoe and I exchanged a look, and I nodded. "All right, then. The predictions I make with my typewriter," I said, "there's no rhyme or reason to them. They just...hit me, all at once, and whenever they feel like it. I thought witches were supposed to control their own powers, not be at the mercy of them." I pursed my lips. As much of a win as the last two bouts of inspiration had been, the nagging frustration was still there, along with a sense of inadequacy. "Maude tells me about a giraffe escaping the zoo, but *doesn't* warn me that I'm going to end up on the wrong side of the hangman's noose? And then some are super vague, and others so specific. Why does it take a crisis or a potion just to get this magic to work?"

Connie's eyes were full of sympathy and she gave me a gentle smile. "Ah, yes. Once you realized you were able to influence the result by saving your grandmother after her heart attack, they became more vague. That's a good step. Those prophecies seem weaker but are actually much stronger because you can take action, effect change and alter the outcome. It's difficult to master but these things take time, Cricket. You're only just coming into your power. Often, it can take witches months, if not years, to truly step into their abilities. You should be proud of how far you've come in such a short time. Just try to be patient. I wish I could say more, but..."

She began to cough, a harsh, barking noise that made it sound like her throat was closing up.

Eyes wide, I put a hand on her back, hardly able to stand watching her wheeze like this. "Can we help you, Connie?" I asked. "Is there anything I can do to stop it?"

The other woman just shook her head. "I'm afraid not," she replied with a weak smile.

Zoe winced. "That's the thing. From what I read, spells in general can only be undone by the person who cast them. In this case, I imagine whoever is in possession of the magical item at the Organization is the only one who can free Connie's tongue. Is that right?"

Connie froze, eyes glazed over for a moment before she shook her head fiercely and closed her fingers over my arm. "I can't...Not much time. Ask, child!" she demanded, searing me with her gaze.

"All right, all right," I muttered, growing more frantic by the second. Was she about to switch sides again on us? What were we supposed to do if this lucid moment ended? I was pretty sure Zoe's rolling pin wasn't going to cut it. "What about our ancestors, then? The other witches of Rocky Knoll? What can you tell us about our coven?"

"Gone. All gone, now." I waited for her to elaborate, but she just shook her head helplessly, rubbing the muscles of her throat with slightly trembling fingers.

"Okay," I said. "We can't ask about specifics to do with our coven or our family." I glanced over at Patrick, who was still watching the exchange in surly silence from the corner of the room. "What do you know about what they did to her?"

Patrick shook his head, sitting up. "Not much. The Organization found out she had possession of at least one magical item, and was on the move toward this town. We had already identified Rocky Knoll as a hotspot."

"A 'hotspot'?" I asked, furrowing my brow.

Patrick nodded. "It's our word for a place with an unusual level of magical activity. In this case, three witches at once, giving off a low-level magical pulse that we were able to detect with our own technology." He shifted a little in his seat, his gaze locking with mine for a brief moment. "We came here to monitor the process, and once the first witch, *you,* was reconnected with her item, my father took measures to make sure that Connie didn't make contact with the second witch until after you had already been separated from your item."

"Why, though?" I asked. "What was the point of that?"

"The Organization can't afford for all three witches to come into their magic at once," Patrick replied. "That would make you too powerful for us to handle. As for Connie, I was told she was under surveillance to keep a tight rein on things. But the night you were kidnapped…That was when I realized it went deeper than that."

His eyes drifted back to Connie, who was looking paler by the minute, practically a husk of her former self. The spell had clearly taken a toll, a fact that Patrick definitely noted, judging by his pained expression. The guilt of his involvement was eating him up.

"I…didn't realize the lengths the Organization would go to," he went on, his voice tight with barely repressed anger. "I didn't know they would employ the magical items in their possession already, in the way they supposedly despised most. Using someone like a puppet…it's unforgivable."

Swallowing hard, I turned back to Connie. "Why didn't they just imprison you, then? Or kill you?"

"Her presence in the town was necessary," Patrick said. "They needed her to reunite you with your magical items. They know the witches are here in Rocky Knoll, but they don't know what the items are until they're in the hands of their true owner."

"That explains why Zoe was able to take the cauldron from your shop," I observed, looking over at my cousin. "Connie only flipped her switch and started chasing us after you already had it."

"Well, what about the cauldron?" Zoe piped up. "I spent all day trying to get it to work, but the only successful potion I made wasn't a potion at all. It was a plate of cinnamon rolls. What's the deal with that?"

"Potions aren't a straightforward craft," Connie explained, looking relieved when the words flowed freely. "Recipes, to some extent, are unique to the person brewing them. It's about intention, and using the ingredients that *feel* right," she continued. "Continue to develop your skills while you search for the final item."

"Welp," Mee-maw said, putting her hands on her hips, "we'd better find this third witch, first, or the item is useless to us anyway. How do we know the Organization hasn't already gotten their hands on it, or her?"

Sharp as a tack, and yet the most obvious things still found a way of going over her head sometimes. I looked from my grandmother to Connie's confused expression.

Here we go...

"In order to protect the coven as a whole," Connie said, "I kept two of the items in my possession. The third is still h--" But she choked on the last word, another fit of wheezing taking her over as I moved to pat her on the back.

"Gotcha. Okay. So, sort of like Voldemort with the horcruxes in *Harry Potter,*" Zoe chimed in with a sage nod. "You had to keep them separated."

"As far as the identity of the third witch, though..." Slowly, Connie turned to look at Mee-maw with a pointed stare.

Mee-maw looked from Connie, to Zoe, to me, and back to Connie, her eyes suddenly widening.

"Oh. Oh! Well, slap my bottom and call me Sally. It's me, isn't it?"

CHAPTER 9

I squeezed my eyes closed and swallowed a groan as chaos ensued. It wasn't like I'd expected to keep the news under wraps forever, but I'd hoped for at least another day to think about how to approach sharing the big news.

First and most importantly, Mee-maw had endured more than eight decades on this earth, and every single one of them had taken a toll on her body. Granted, she was more spry than a lot of people her age but if the past couple weeks had proven anything, it was that she wasn't as strong as she used to be. We'd brought her into the loop out of necessity, knowing that if the doo-doo hit the fan, we could sideline her, like when Zoe and I had gone to Connie's shop and gotten hunted down. Now that she knew she was a witch?

Not even a Sherman tank would stop her.

"Wow...that's...huge," Zoe murmured, shaking her head as she glanced my way, eyes wide with panic.

"Whoo hoo! I mean, I guess it makes sense, but who'da thunk it?" Mee-maw demanded, eyes glittering with excitement as she regarded Connie with a wide grin. "So, lay it on me! What are my special powers? I can't wait to hear it."

Connie touched a finger to her lips and shook her head.

"Can't say, right?" Mee-maw confirmed with a sage nod. "Roger that. Well, that's okay. Me and my coven, here, we'll figure it out ourselves. Thanks for telling us. Who knows when we'd have figured it out without you! Right, girls?"

I stole a guilty glance at Patrick but he was studying his fingernails intently as Zoe and Mee-maw turned toward me with a frown.

"Um, yeah. So about that..." I swallowed hard and opened my mouth to fess up. "Patrick knew for a while now."

It hadn't been exactly what I'd planned to say, but given the scowl Mee-maw was aiming at Patrick, I couldn't bring myself to walk it back, either.

"You knew?" Mee-maw demanded, cocking a hand on one hip. "Why the Moses didn't you tell me?"

Patrick hesitated long enough to shoot me a glare, and then raked a hand through his dark hair.

"I didn't *know*. I just suspected. And honestly, it doesn't even matter. We don't know what your item is and, until you have it, any powers will remain dormant just as they have for the past forty years or so when you could've come into your power."

Connie nodded in agreement. "A crone's coven is--" She snapped her mouth shut, her eyes going wide. "They're returning! I need to go. Most importantly, a warning. Do not try to contact me going forward. For all intents and purposes, I am enemy number one."

She wheeled around and hightailed it back toward the cellar door like the hounds of hell were hot on her heels.

I followed her down the stairs, calling after her, but by the time I got there, she was gone, as if she'd never even been there.

"Crap."

I rushed to the open window and caught sight of her flowing caftan as she rounded the corner.

"She would've stayed and helped more if she could've," Patrick observed softly from behind me.

I turned, surprised to see him standing at the bottom of the stairs. For such a sizable hunk of man, he was awfully stealthy.

"Yeah, I know. I just hoped I could ask her a couple more questions, is all. I guess we have to assume by 'they're returning' she means the Organization's little pep rally is over and they're on their way back to Rocky Knoll to continue their attempted murder spree?"

He inclined his dark head, a ghost of a smile tugging at his firm lips. "That's a safe enough assumption, I'd say. As I've mentioned, they have ways of detecting a coven in a general location, so we knew we only had a little bit of a head start to get back here and settle in somewhere. I'd hoped for more time, but it is what it is. At least we have advanced warning of their arrival."

"I guess," I said, sparing one last glance at the window before closing it.

"We can talk more about it before we turn in for the night. I'm going to board this window first."

"Sounds good. And hey, sorry about the whole Mee-maw thing and throwing you under the bus." I chewed on the inside of my cheek as I tried to think of a good explanation, but he saved me the trouble.

"Oh, yeah, no worries. She's terrifying. I'd have done the same."

That got a tiny grin out of me and some of my unrest melted away.

We'd made good progress. Zoe had managed to make a real potion of sorts with her cinnamon buns—albeit not on command when she was actually trying to make one, but still. I didn't have to worry about hiding anything from Mee-maw and

Zoe, and we'd learned some helpful, if incomplete, information from Connie.

Best of all, though, I was reconnected with Maude again. Not bad for a day's work.

"Uh, Houston?" Zoe's voice echoed down the stairway. "We've got a problem."

My stomach sank and I squeezed my eyes closed with a sigh.

When would I learn to stop looking for silver linings? All it seemed to do was make it pour again.

"Coming up in a sec," I called back.

I scrounged around for a hammer and nails and Patrick made quick work of boarding the window with an oversized scrap of plywood. Then, we headed upstairs, with me praying under my breath that whatever had gone wrong this time wasn't a critical blow to our progress.

"What's up?" Patrick asked as we stepped back into the kitchen.

Mee-maw jerked a thumb at a clearly upset Zoe. "Gina Lollobrigida over here is losing her beauty boost. And I gotta admit, my sciatica is starting to throb a little again."

Zoe nodded mournfully, gesturing to her face. "My age spot is coming back. It's light right now, but I think we can see where this is headed."

The cinnamon bun magic was temporary, which meant...

"Maude!"

I rushed to the table and dropped into the chair in front of the typewriter, a burst of adrenaline mixed with fear coursing through my veins. "Someone, get me another one of those buns, stat!"

I sucked in a steadying breath and let my fingers hover over the keys again. Then, I waited for the tingle to start or the hot flash to wash over me.

"Come on, come on!" I glanced at Zoe and noted that her

hair hadn't changed back yet, and a quick perusal of Mee-maw confirmed that her skin was still rosy and pink with vigor. Surely, I could get one more prediction out of Maude before the magic wore off.

When the wave of magic finally came, it was weak this time. A flush of heat, and little sizzle down my wrist blooming at my fingertips. A moment later, I was typing...until I wasn't anymore, an all-too brief moment later.

"Dang it," I muttered, staring down at the five words on the page in front of me. "There's got to be more."

Time is ticking. The final

Mee-maw ambled up to the table and shoved a chunk of cinnamon bun into my mouth. Then another, and another, as I chewed furiously. Twenty excruciating minutes and three cinnamon buns later, all I had to show for it was an aching belly and a broken heart. It was confirmed.

Consumed or not, the magic imbued into Zoe's baked goods was temporary.

Which meant Maude and I were separated, with only a silvery thread between us, yet again. Losing it had been terrible. Getting it back and having it taken away again was almost unbearable.

"I don't know if I can do this," I whispered miserably, a fat tear plopping onto the nearly-blank page in front of me. "It's too hard."

I hated being a sad-sack, but I'd reached the bottom of the well. Terror, the sleepless nights, the grief for this inanimate object that somehow felt like a piece of me. I couldn't take it anymore.

I turned to face the others and shrugged helplessly.

"Seriously, someone tell me...What are we doing this all for, anyway? What if we just let them have what they want? Leave the items behind and go hide in Peru or somewhere far away where they can't find us, until they stop looking."

"What about Greg and the kids? What about Phil and my bakery?" Zoe asked gently.

"I don't even habla español," Mee-maw added with a shake of her head. "Plus, I haven't gotten to try out my magic yet."

"More importantly, if we *could* leave and take our families along, our items are useless to the Organization without the three of us, and yours would only follow you like it always has," Zoe said, ignoring Mee-maw and pressing on. "You think they're ever going to stop trying to find us until they get what they want?"

She was right and I knew it, but dang it, this was feeling more and more like a losing battle. One that was going to end the same way, no matter what we did.

With me swinging from a rope and my sister-cousin and my grandmother not far behind.

"I wish I knew what the hell I was doing," I said, slumping over Maude and pressing my cheek to her keys. "I'm so sick of being in the dark."

A silence fell over the room for a long moment.

"So let's focus on what we do know, all right?" Zoe urged, pulling up a chair beside mine as Mee-maw and Patrick followed suit. "The Organization's goal, as I understand it to this point, is to reunite each of us with our item, allow us time to charge them with magic, then capture us so they can separate us from our items and kill us. But they can't do it all at once. Which means they are going to be looking to do several things. Number one," she brandished a finger, "recapture Cricket, kill her, and take Maude. Number two," she flicked up a second finger, "ensure that I don't get killed in the process, because they need me to continue building the power of the cauldron. And number three," she chunked up the trifecta, "keep Mee-maw's item from her until they have dealt with Cricket and I. That sort of makes our path pretty clear now, doesn't it?"

Nothing seemed clear to me in that moment, but I lifted my head up and tried to follow what she was saying as Patrick and Mee-maw nodded.

"If they're all hot and bothered about us having them at the same time, that means they're afraid. They know that, together, as a coven, we can bring down the whole danged Organization. It's a race," Mee-maw said with a chuckle. "A race for Cricket to reconnect with Maude for good, Zoe to get a handle on her powers, and me to find my item before they can nab Cricket again. Sound about right, Patrick?"

Patrick tipped his head. "Sounds right to me."

I ran a gentle hand over Maude's keys and swiped the single tear from the sheet of paper.

"Where do we even start?"

"Let's get to know our enemy a little more," Zoe suggested, turning to Patrick. "Patrick can help with that."

"I am happy to tell you everything I know, but understand that it's far less than you might imagine. I had no idea what they were capable of or their true intentions."

"Facts only, then," Zoe said with a shrug. "Stuff you've seen with your own eyes."

My mind drifted back to that terrible night and I swallowed past the sudden tightness in my throat. "When I was imprisoned, the man they had guarding me was wearing a necklace."

I hadn't been able to bring myself to even think on it for too long, never mind discuss it with the others, but it was important, so I had to muscle through.

"It was magic. He was able to use it to bring pain." A cold sweat broke out on my upper lip and I swiped it away.

"Indescribable, unimaginable pain. The type of pain that would break a person."

"Geez, Crick..." Zoe leaned in, looking heartsick.

Mee-maw scowled and patted my hand awkwardly. "I hope my item is a wand so when I see Finneas I can shove it right up his--"

"You won't need to do that," Patrick snarled, his face a mask of fury. "I'll take care of my father. He'll pay for what he did to you, Cricket. And for the lies he's told."

"Look, you guys," I said, holding up both hands. "I didn't tell you about the necklace to make you mad. I brought it up because we know they have already procured other magical items. The one that allowed them to tongue-tie Connie and possess her. There are others, to be sure. If we had an idea of what some of them did, maybe we can protect ourselves against them and prepare a little better."

"Good point," Mee-maw said. "Patrick, what others do you know of?"

"I can tell you that I didn't know about that one," he said, shaking his head miserably. "I imagine my father knew if I'd been aware of something so evil, I'd have advocated destroying it immediately. But I do know of a few others. There is a hand mirror that reveals the true intentions of the person looking into it."

Mee-maw let out a low whistle. "That's a good one. Probably keeps them from getting double-crossed or infiltrated."

"It's used sparingly. Keep in mind, without the witch owner to recharge the magic, all the items are slowly drained of power as they're used. They also have a jewelry box. You put something inside, and close the box. When you open it again, it has been turned into gemstones or precious metal."

Zoe shook her head slowly. "Nice. Hence their deep pockets. They have endless funds."

"And then there's the candlestick." His expression went dark. "It's supposed to allow the user to commune with the dead. To my knowledge, that one has never been utilized, despite being in the Organization's hands for a long time. Organization leaders are too afraid of what they might unleash into the world. Aside from the charged items, there is a vault that houses dozens of items that have been used up, as well as others that they believe are magic but remain dormant. They keep them in an underground bunker in Milan in the event that they locate the owner's ancestors and are able to recharge them some day."

"That's it? Those are all the active items you can think of?"

Patrick nodded. "And, again, they don't use them all that often. Both due to waning strength and because it requires lots of red tape and authorization, for obvious reasons. If the item were lost or stolen, it would be able to be used by anyone, unchecked."

That was good to know and a definite plus for our side. If we could all get our items and connect with them, we were an endless source of power.

Too bad that was a big "if".

"What else do you know to be true, beyond a shadow of a doubt?" I asked softly.

"Just that Mee-maw is right. They're scared," Patrick said, his face solemn. "Terrified at the thought of you getting your powers back and solidifying the coven. There is also no doubt in my mind that the Organization needs to operate under the radar. They don't want the government to catch wind of any of this. Can you imagine what this would mean for national security? If a country figured out how to weaponize some of these items..." He trailed off with a shrug. "Chaos. They work in shadows."

"So let's not make it easy for them," I said, a crazy idea

floating to the forefront of my brain as one of the lines from Maude's recent premonitions came rushing back. "Let's make sure that, when they do come for us, it's an ugly, chaotic, mess."

Turn on the kitchen light and the cockroaches scatter.

I picked up the bakery landline as the others watched me, a mix of curiosity and worry etched on their faces.

I dialed a number and waited. A moment later, a woman picked up.

"Rocky Knoll Sheriff's office, this is Judy, how can I help you?"

"Hi, Judy," I said, hearing the trembling in my voice but unable to make it stop. "I need to report a kidnapping and attempted murder."

CHAPTER 10

THE WAIT for the cops to arrive was tense. I was sitting in the front room of the bakery, my eyes flitting to the door every other moment, while Zoe leaned against the counter and Mee-maw slouched in a chair, tapping away on one of the burner phones. Patrick was leaning against the far wall, his shoulders hunched and his arms crossed over his chest, looking wound up.

He hadn't been a hundred percent sold on the idea, at first. It felt like a Hail Mary, and I knew it, but my intuition was telling me it was the right move. If this would help us slow the Organization down, even a little, then it would be worth it. All we needed was time. The key was giving the cops just enough information to give us what we wanted and poke around a little, but not so much that they successfully hunted the members down and engaged.

There'd been more than enough blood spilled already. I refused to send clueless, innocent people into the clutches of Finneas Byrne and his mini-army of magic-stealing fanatics.

Without magic, it wasn't a fair fight.

"What are you doing, Mee-maw?" Zoe asked, sounding antsy.

"Texting Trudy," Mee-maw replied without looking up. "Keeping her updated."

"Are you sure that's a good idea?" Zoe bit her lip. "I mean, I get that she wants to help us, but--"

"She hasn't given us any reason not to trust her yet. We can't afford to be picky right now."

"Mm. I guess that's true." Zoe pushed away from the counter, crossing her arms. "I just hate this. I thought with the Organization in New York we'd at least have a little more time."

"We're just going to have to find a way to outsmart them," Mee-maw replied. "We've done a bang-up job so far, if I do say so myself. And once I've got the powers of the universe at my command..." She raised her head, a wicked grin spreading across her face. "We'll be unstoppable."

"All right, all right. Take it easy, Dumbledore," Zoe murmured. "We don't even have your item yet."

At that moment, there was a knock at the door.

We all exchanged a look and I took a deep breath before padding over and taking a furtive peek around the shade in place over the glass. Two uniformed police officers stood waiting. I made quick work of the locks and pushed the door open, the little bell giving off a tinkling ring.

My heart sank when the two stepped in and I recognized the first as Mitch Rasmusson. The lanky officer with the rust-colored hair was the other half of my former classmate, Marilee, a woman who was twice as nosy as she was grating. We'd all gone to school together and, while I didn't dislike him, I didn't love the idea of having to unload my tale on someone whose wife was a modern version of the town crier.

The other cop was a fit guy in his early fifties with sandy hair, who I didn't recognize off the bat. I noted that he was wearing a sheriff's badge, which I supposed was a good sign. Might as well start at the top.

"Evening," Deputy Rasmusson said, hooking his thumbs into his belt loops. "Cricket." He nodded to me, and then to Zoe. "Zoe."

"What am I, chopped liver?" Mee-maw demanded, sitting up in her chair.

I shot her a warning look. "Thank you for coming, Officers. I know the dispatcher mentioned, typically, if a crime didn't just happen that we would go in to file a report, but I think you'll understand why that wasn't possible, in this case."

"Not a problem, Ma'am. We go where we need to in order to get the job done," said the sheriff, extending a hand first to me and then to the others. "Sheriff Colton Webber. Been on the job about two years now but don't think I've had the pleasure of meeting you all yet."

Zoe was already devouring him with her eyes. "I know I haven't met *you*, Sheriff. I'd have remembered."

Sheriff Webber blinked, but I saw the ghost of a smile appear on his face. "Well," he replied, adjusting his tie, "I appreciate that, ma'am."

I shared a glance with Patrick, hardly able to resist rolling my eyes. Here we were, on the run from a shadowy organization, and Zoe was flirting.

Deputy Rasmusson cleared his throat. "Anyway. If you folks wouldn't mind giving us a statement about what happened. Judy in dispatch said attempted murder?"

The sheriff blinked, coming back to himself, and nodded. "Yes, you must be very shaken up by all this. Shall we take a seat and you can run us through what happened?"

I motioned for them to join us in the kitchen, where we all took seats. Deputy Rasmusson produced a recording device.

"Why don't you start at the beginning," he suggested. "Which one of you was the intended victim?"

I swallowed hard and raised my hand. Talking about this to

Patrick and the others was one thing, but bringing it to the attention of normal people—skeptics—was an entirely different ballgame. I couldn't help feeling a little self-conscious, even though we'd already planned out our story, down to the last detail.

"I was kidnapped, three nights ago," I began, "although, it's all sort of a blur. I was minding my own business, just taking a nice evening stroll, and they nabbed me right off the street. Tossed a hood over my head, threw me into the back of a van of some kind. They drove me to a remote location where they--" I didn't have to fake the emotion choking me now. "They were insane—they took my phone, threw me in a cell. They tortured me, and then they tried to kill me. It was some kind of...ritual or something. They tried to hang me. If these guys hadn't shown up, I would've died."

"A cult?" Rasmusson frowned. "What kind of cult are we talking about, here?"

I cleared my throat. "They, ah..." I glanced at Patrick for support, and he gave me a reassuring nod. "They seem to think that Zoe, my grandma and I are evil witches."

"Witches." The deputy raised an eyebrow. "As in, cauldrons and broomsticks?"

I chewed the inside of my lip. "It sounds crazy, I know."

Rasmusson heaved a heavy sigh. "You mentioned on the phone that you've been hiding out here—you said you think these people might be watching your houses. Is that correct?" I nodded, and he turned to Zoe, who was leaning in close to Sheriff Webber on the other side of the counter.

"Marilee mentioned that Cricket was in the midst of a divorce." *Of course she did.* "But what about your husband?" Rasmusson asked Zoe, drawing the sheriff's attention momentarily back—although, not without some difficulty. "Is he staying here, too?"

Zoe shook her head. "He's out of town," she replied. "He'll be gone for another two days."

The deputy shot her a suspicious glance. "A killer cult on the loose, and he's away on business?"

"I'm planning on telling him when he gets home," Zoe replied, a little defensively. "We each value our independence, so it's not unusual for us to go a couple days without talking," she added, with a glance toward the sheriff. "Plus, I don't want him to freak out and come rushing back. We *certainly* don't want another person for us to worry about involved in this mess, if we can help it."

"She does have a point," Sheriff Webber said, giving Zoe a small smile, which she eagerly reciprocated.

The deputy turned back to us, muttering something under his breath. He wasn't sold. That was okay. We just needed him to buy in a little bit.

"Why are you just reporting this now?"

"Because we were on the run before," Mee-maw piped in with a sniff.

"Of course," he said with a tight smile. "And were you all there to witness this?" he asked dubiously.

"No. We went to rescue her." Mee-maw was getting irritated now and she shot to her feet with a wince. "She has the injuries to prove it. Show 'em, Cricket."

I'd expected this and nodded, tugging down the collar of my shirt to display the mark from the rope. It was largely faded now, almost gone, but a yellow-greenish bruise still remained. Next, I lifted the hem of my shirt to reveal the gnarly, raised scar where I had been stabbed, with a line of stitches marching down the length of it.

It was enough to make the deputy balk a little. "Did you go to the hospital?"

Patrick shook his head. "I was able to patch her up." There was a pause, and he added, "I've had some first aid training."

"Uh-huh." I could see the incredulity on the deputy's face, and my heart sank. "So you're telling me you were stabbed and hanged, and you *didn't* go to the hospital?"

"What? So they could've found us there to finish the job?" Mee-maw shot back.

I glanced over at Zoe, who had given the sheriff a croissant at some point, that he was now chewing thoughtfully. He seemed to be buying it more than Rasmusson, at least, who was looking from me to Mee-maw to Patrick with raised eyebrows.

The deputy sighed. "With all due respect, Ms. Hawthorne, that cut looks at least a week old. And--"

"Wait a minute," Mee-maw interjected, "I can back this all up, and so can the others. We were all there—we saved her from the noose, dang it!"

"That's all well and good," Deputy Rasmusson said, "but you *do* understand how absurd this all sounds, don't you? This is Rocky Knoll, not New Orleans during Mardi Gras. Things like this just don't happen here."

This was enough to make Mee-maw's eyes flash. "Listen here, sonny. I went to school with your grandmother, so stop rolling your eyes at my granddaughter and listen, unless you want blood on your hands," she said, stepping forward and brandishing a finger at the deputy. "People everywhere, small town or big city, are capable of evil."

Rasmusson balked a little, taken aback. "Apologies. I just...I need to get my head around all of this. Why you? Why now?"

I pursed my lips. "It's all right. Look..." I crossed my arms. "These people have been after me for a while, now. They're dangerous, and they're still looking for us. This goes beyond just me, here. What we need is protection. Someone to keep them from coming in here and trying again. If we don't, I feel like something terrible is going to happen."

He must have heard the solemn sincerity in those words because he nodded slowly. "All right. Can you describe any of these cult members?"

We'd already decided not to share Finneas's name and keep it vague, for their own protection.

"Not really. It was dark, and--"

"Right," Rasmusson said with a smirk.

"They were wearing hoods, as well," Patrick added smoothly. "But I swear to you, Officer, they were all-too real."

And just like that, the deputy's expression lost all signs of skepticism. "So you're saying you tracked these kidnappers," he said, his eyes fixed on Patrick, "and you saw this all happen. Can you tell me about that, in your own words?"

Patrick went on to repeat our version of the events, and then went quiet.

"Well, now, this is troubling," Rasmusson said. "It sounds almost like a human sacrifice."

"That's exactly what it was," Patrick confirmed, nodding.

It was something to behold; the deputy seemed darn near entranced by what Patrick was saying, hanging on every word, even though I had already given him the exact same story only moments ago. It was like, only now, as Patrick was telling it, did it have any credence whatsoever.

The freaking patriarchy, I thought, shaking my head. *I tell him what happened, and he's all eyerolls. When another guy tells it, he's like, "Okay, we'll get right on it!"*

I looked back over at the counter, where Zoe was rattling off the same details to Sheriff Webber, who was nodding intently, his eyes never leaving hers. He was falling for it—and her— hook, line, and sinker. At least she was having an easier time with all this.

"And you say you were able to find her because of an app on your phone?" Rasmusson confirmed with Patrick.

He nodded. "We tracked her to this abandoned factory. I can give you the general location and maybe you can go have a look? They've surely scattered, but it might be worth looking for evidence—maybe it will help us figure out where they've gone."

Another calculated risk. They wouldn't leave us a guard without an active case in progress, so we needed to give them some leads and Patrick had confirmed what we'd all assumed to be true. There was no way the Organization hadn't cleared out the factory and hightailed out of there directly after my escape.

"Yes," Rasmusson said, nodding, "I can go check it out myself." He turned to the sheriff, who was just wrapping up with Zoe. "All good?"

"Oh, yes," Sheriff Webber replied, winking—actually *winking*—at Zoe as he turned around. "We'll open up a case file right away. If you folks see anything suspicious, I want you to report it, all right? No more waiting this time."

I nodded. "Got it."

"But in the meantime," Patrick spoke up as the men turned to leave. Here it was. The big ask. "Cricket mentioned protection. Would it be possible to at least have someone out in front here, just to keep an eye on the place? They're going to come back. They're going to try their best to finish what they started. These people are crazy..."

The two cops exchanged a look. Rasmusson shrugged and the Sheriff nodded.

"That's not a bad idea. My guess is, they won't be back. Things didn't work the way they'd hoped, and they're long gone, but better safe than sorry. It's a slow time of year right now...We'll have an officer posted in the strip mall to keep an eye out while we work the case over the next couple days. I can't promise anything longer-term, though. Unless we find hard evidence of a crime, we can't commit the resources. Does that work for you?"

"Yes," Patrick replied. "That would be perfect."

I let out a sigh of relief.

The bakery would be just a little safer now.

"You folks are going to all stay here? There's also a safehouse about thirty miles away in Mission's Port we might be able to arrange--"

"That won't be necessary," Zoe interrupted with a smile. "We'll be staying here for now." Webber frowned, but shrugged his broad shoulders. "All right, then," he said. "Whatever helps you all feel safe. I'll send someone over in the next hour or so." He nodded to Deputy Rasmusson. "That about covers it. We'll keep you in the loop if we find out anything, but we want you to keep *us* in the loop, too. Deal?"

"Deal," I said, nodding, and reached out to shake the sheriff's hand. "Thank you again, Officers."

"Our pleasure," Sheriff Webber replied, tipping his hat to us before holding the door open for Rasmusson, who left without a word.

We were left looking at one another as the patrol car pulled out of the parking lot. "That went better than I was expecting," I said at last. "You've really got a way with words, Patrick. He was sold the second you explained everything."

The big man rubbed the back of his neck. "It's our lucky day."

Mee-maw, who had been quietly studying her phone screen, suddenly looked up, her eyes wide. "Hot dog! You're not kidding."

"What is it?" Patrick asked, turning to her.

"Trudy," Mee-maw replied.

In addition to calling the cops, in keeping with Maude's prediction about trust and safety in numbers, we'd agreed to let the librarian in on the whole truth. She'd been gobsmacked and didn't question a word of what we'd told her. All she wanted to do was help.

"She just messaged me back—she thinks she has a way of getting you your powers back permanently, Cricket."

"Really?" My eyes widened. Great news, if true, although by now, I was learning not to get too optimistic. Mee-maw nodded eagerly.

"Well, what are we waiting for?" Zoe demanded. "What does she need from us?"

"Yeah, about that..." replied Mee-maw, fidgeting.

I might have audibly groaned. There was always a catch. "Spill it."

I watched my grandmother roll her shoulders back, a determined air settling over her. "Better get the Mystery Machine ready," she said with a grim smile. "We're meeting her at midnight tonight...in the Rocky Knoll Cemetery."

Of course we were.

CHAPTER 11

An owl hooted as we stepped past another row of gravestones in the dim light of Trudy's old-timey lantern, only adding to the horrible sense of fear that permeated our group.

We'd had to sneak out the back of the bakery and walk halfway to the graveyard in the dark before Trudy picked us up, but I'd been right to relish the extra time to prepare. Being in a graveyard at this time of night, with the nagging thought that we were being hunted, was *not* pleasant.

Being in one like this? Made it a thousand times worse.

The cemetery wasn't of the modern variety, with sleek, shiny stones made of rose gold quartz with manicured grounds where Easter lilies planted by loved ones dotted the landscape.

This was an old school graveyard, down a winding, narrow road, butted up next to a creepy forest. The kind with cracked, hand-cobbled tombstones, surrounded by hulking trees with gnarled branches that looked a little too much like claws for my taste.

The moon hung, fat and round in the sky, as a gust of autumn wind sent those spooky trees a-waving.

"Are we close?" I whispered, getting more anxious by the second.

"Yup. Just up ahead," Trudy said, pointing at a patch of tombstones, slightly removed from the rest and with a few open spaces where photos that Mee-maw had found confirmed the graves of our ancestors had once rested.

I pushed my fear aside as we approached the open spots where stones should've been.

"So what do we do?" I asked, looking to Trudy, who was pulling something out of the pocket of a robe that looked like she'd stolen from the Druids or one of those sand people from Star Wars. I stifled a chuckle, pretending not to notice as she batted at the hem of her sleeve, which had caught fire from the lantern she held in her other hand.

I had to give her credit for going the full monty.

"Ah, here we go," she said, sounding composed even as she glanced around to see if anyone had noticed. She set down her lantern and held out a handful of papers, proffering them to each of us in turn.

I grabbed one, handling it delicately when I noticed the yellowish tint of age that covered the page and the ancient font that the text was written in. "How old are these?"

"Why does this smell like Earl Grey?" Mee-maw asked before Trudy could answer, sniffing hers.

"They're from, like, an hour ago?" she replied with a sage nod. "And the tea thing was for ambience. You just wet the bags and rub them on the--" Trudy broke off at our stares. "Forgive me for trying to get us in the spirit, here," she said, holding up her hands defensively.

"I think it's a nice touch," Mee-maw said with a curt nod. "If you're gonna do something, do it right."

Trudy beamed at her and then cleared her throat.

"All right, back to business. Let's all read to ourselves for a second to get the cadence of the text first."

I glanced back at the paper to see that it was just regular computer paper with a short chant, almost like a prayer, typed out on it in flowery letters. "So we just say this together?"

"Yes," Trudy said, herding us like children into a semicircle around the three open spots where gravestones had once stood, before placing her lantern in the center. She'd put the three of us in the center with Patrick on our left before walking to her own spot on the far right. "We may have to repeat it a few times, but I have it on good authority that this chant will reconnect you with the magic of your ancestors."

I nodded, wondering if her idea of an authority was as tenuous as Mee-maw's when she was going on about her conspiracy theories. I'd have liked to think a librarian would be a little more discerning but it was hard to expect much from someone who was as into the Illuminati stuff as she was. It wasn't like anyone had any better ideas, though.

Patrick, who had been silent and visibly uncomfortable since we'd walked through the gate, finally piped up. "Maybe I should go stand at the entrance and keep watch?"

Mee-maw silenced him with a glare, going full Warden-mode as she snapped, "You'll stand here and like it, young man, with all that you owe the three of us. You're lucky I haven't smacked you upside the head for what you did to my granddaughter, so don't push your luck."

I couldn't help but chuckle as he looked back down at the page without a word. Mee-maw's tongue had dulled some with age but a dull knife was still a knife, after all.

"Let us begin," Trudy said, beginning to chant slowly, her eyes closed.

The rest of us followed suit, droning the incomprehensible,

vaguely latin-sounding, words along with her. It was super awkward at first, and I found myself opening one eye and locking gazes with a slightly skeptical-looking Zoe about halfway through the first recitation. Soon enough, though, a strange sense of calm seemed to blanket us and the otherwise-terrifying graveyard.

A sense of calm that still hadn't amounted to anything more as we completed the chant for the dozenth time.

"I don't want to be a downer, team, but what's the plan now?" Zoe said with a sigh. "Don't you think it would have worked by now if it was going to?"

"We started a couple minutes early. Let's try just a few more times," Trudy said, looking embarrassed as she closed her eyes and leading us into the chant again.

It struck me all at once how creepy this was and how bad this would look if anyone saw us. A group of witches chanting spells that were probably found on an internet forum in the middle of a graveyard? How freaking cliché could we get?

Those thoughts faded quickly, however, and were replaced with a strange feeling of something else. Like a shift in the very fabric of the world.

As if something broken was becoming whole again as a puzzle piece clicked into place.

I tried to say something...let the others know what I was feeling, but the sensation was too overwhelming, rendering me speechless.

I let the paper in my hands fall to the ground, staring at the grass in front of me. I was strangely drawn to it as I stepped forward, feeling more like a spectator to my body's actions than the one actually controlling them as I dropped to my knees.

In the distance somewhere, I thought I heard frantic voices calling my name. I couldn't make out what any of them were saying, their words seeming as foreign as the chant. In an all-too rare moment of stunning clarity, I knew what to do as surely as I knew how to tie my shoes. Magic flowed through my body as the world around me came alive.

I could feel the breath of the trees.

Sense the elation of the owl as it swooped down with open talons to snatch its midnight snack from the grass.

Smell the sweet flora and musky fauna teeming in the nearby forest.

But most of all, I could feel them. My ancestors. Their wisdom. Their power. Their love.

A sparkling image of Maude floated to the forefront of my mind, and even though she was miles away, safe at the bakery, I could sense the wavering arc between us. Our link, fragile and thin, but still there. On instinct, I *heaved* with all my strength, feeling a strange sense of relief as the ground began to tremble beneath me.

My previously riotous world went silent for a moment and I opened my eyes, coming back into myself. I realized in that moment that I was on the ground, and tried frantically to stand, slightly dizzy and super disoriented.

Patrick shouted my name, jerking me to my feet but I didn't even turn to look at him as I stumbled and stood. What was in front of us was too wonderful.

An ornate mausoleum with gilded doors had erupted from the ground and pushed its way from the soil and grass.

"There's more," Trudy hissed in awe.

She was right. Two other mausoleums rose from the ground in a shower of dirt and pebbles and earthworms to flank the first.

"Holy mackerel," Mee-maw said, her eyes wide.

"I guess that chant of yours had something to it after all, Trudy," Zoe said, looking appreciatively at the librarian. "Well done, friend. Thank you."

"Of course," Trudy said, standing a little taller. "You're so welcome. So glad to help."

Whether it was the chant itself or just our presence here in our ancestral burial grounds, we wouldn't have come if not for Trudy. I wanted to melt with relief that my instinct in trusting her hadn't been wrong.

I contemplated the mausoleums for a long moment and then nodded, certain of what we were supposed to do next.

"We need to go inside." I felt drawn to the mausoleum in the center like a moth to a flame, and each second we waited to enter felt like a mild form of torture.

"I'll keep watch," Patrick said, furrowing his brow, his face as white as a sheet as the muscle in his jaw ticked.

There was no time to worry about his anxiety around magic. All that mattered right now was seeing what was inside that darned tomb. I looked up to see that Zoe and Mee-maw were already just about to step into the two flanking mine.

"Meet back here soon," Zoe said, an almost glazed look in her eyes as she ran her hand lovingly over the stone of the mausoleum she stood before.

"Don't you think we should check them out one by one, in case--" Trudy began, looking around, but it was too late. Mee-maw and Zoe had already pulled the trigger even as I felt myself walking toward the one in the center, as if on autopilot.

"Stay with me, Trudy," I said, pushing the golden door open. The second I stepped in, though, I regretted the invitation. It felt wrong to have someone else in here. Like allowing someone to read your diary. I pushed the feeling aside, relieved as Trudy's lantern revealed the interior.

I stilled, surprised to find a fairly bland room that was empty, save the stone casket in the back. I winced as the stone door to the mausoleum slammed shut with a grinding *thud*.

"Whoa," Trudy whispered.

I was about to respond when I realized that everything had

changed. The tomb that had been no more than seven or eight feet tall and ten square feet big had opened up into a massive space the size of a house, but with a higher ceiling. Beautiful tapestries adorned the walls, and golden vases and bric a brac that clearly hadn't been touched by the passage of time littered the floor.

Whoever my ancestor was, she'd had a rather gaudy sense of style.

"Unreal."

"I can't believe this is happening," Trudy squeaked, jumping up and down in excitement before rushing to one of the bookshelves that now lined the walls.

I pushed down the part of me that still felt wrong having someone else digging through the stuff in here, *my* stuff, and walked toward the very back end of the tomb. There, a drab, stone altar lay, with a small ceramic vase on top that contained a single black rose. Though it was the least flashy thing in the room, I'd never seen anything as perfect and beautiful in my life. The altar was dimpled with three indents, two in the shape of circles of different sizes on the sides and a large rectangle in the middle.

I stepped up with bated breath, knowing the flower was real and alive before I even touched it. I took a deep pull of its fruity, sweet scent and stood in front of it for a few moments before breaking from my trance as I noticed a wooden box protruding from a hole in the wall just behind the altar. My hands shook as I opened it to find a sturdy-looking compass, its dull, jet-black paint unmarred by the passage of time. I lifted it from its resting place, on a whim, checking to see if it fit inside the smaller circle on the altar.

When it didn't, I slipped it into my pocket reverently.

Mine, a voice from deep inside me whispered.

"Someone is here!"

This voice wasn't internal, and it definitely wasn't a whisper.

"Right now. We have to go!"

Patrick.

"The Organization?" Trudy asked, eyes wide as saucers as I turned to face her.

"I hope not. Look," I said, grabbing her shoulder, speaking in hushed but firm tones, "you stay hidden for now. If it is them, I'll do my best to handle this with my magic. Whatever happened in here tonight, I can feel it inside me now. It will be okay."

She opened her mouth to protest but I cut her off at the pass.

"I know you want to help, and you have. More than you know. But we need to keep you safe. You're too important to our coven for us to lose you now."

It was true. But it was also true that she wouldn't be much use in a fight and her presence could quickly turn into a liability if they managed to take her hostage.

She considered my words for a moment, then lifted her head proudly and nodded. "As you wish, Mistress."

Making a mental note to have a talk with her about the new title, I wheeled around and sprinted to the door. Adrenaline beat a tattoo in my temples as I shoved it open, a prayer on my lips.

Patrick stood a dozen feet ahead of me, bathed in light.

"What do we do?" Zoe hissed.

She and Mee-maw were already outside of their mausoleums with looks of terror on their faces. A cold chill ran through me, followed by a deep nausea as I saw the source of the light. A black SUV with tinted windows had driven onto the cemetery grounds, no regard for running over graves. No respect for the dead. And now, three men were pouring out of the vehicle as the driver slammed his door, striding toward us. A shudder rocked through me as he moved away from the glare of the headlights.

Wiry, tall, black gloves. Sunglasses.

My slim hope that we'd get by with only having to sweet talk the cops and potentially get thrown in the psych ward evaporated as I faced off with the man who had kidnapped me.

"Kill the traitor," the man said.

"But the boss..." One of them balked, pulling back from Patrick for a moment.

"I said, kill him. And then grab the clairvoyant witch. We need her alive to complete the ritual!"

The other man shot me a dubious look.

"We all but severed the link," black gloves snarled in disgust. "Her magic is weak. Don't be a chicken!"

I clenched my fists tight, hoping against hope that he was wrong. The kernel of magic was still inside me somewhere. It'd caught the teacup, after all.

The three men in the back charged toward Patrick, pulling knives from their belts and trying to surround him. I reached for my power, tugging as hard as I could to try to bring it out, but it felt like I was trying to pry open a rusted door.

Patrick turned, as if to run, before exploding off of his front foot, directly toward the closest attacker. The man slashed at him but Patrick was too fast, pushing his arm aside and landing a powerful punch to the man's head, dropping him to the ground.

"Come on, come on, come on!" I whispered as the other two men stepped in, forcing Patrick back from their downed comrade, who showed no sign of getting up. If I didn't get my magic working soon, there was a good chance I'd be watching Patrick die right in front of my eyes.

Patrick dipped in and out of the range of their knives with

agility, landing hits and trying to disarm them, but he was gradually being pushed back. He was putting up a valiant fight but it was clear what the outcome would be, he was just stalling for time.

A soft *click* sounded to my right and saw that Mee-maw was aiming her revolver at the man in the gloves, her hands shaking. "Call them back," she said firmly.

His underlings were too fast, however. Patrick dipped in, landing a strike to one man's arm and preparing to dodge a slice from the other man, but the slice never came. He unleashed a savage kick instead, striking Patrick right on his kneecap. He and his partner leapt on him, with one holding a knife to his throat, knees on his arms, and the other handled his legs.

Their leader smiled. "Drop the gun."

I heard the *clunk* as it hit the ground but my eyes were already closed, a calmness spreading through my body as I prepared to unleash my magic on them. Zoe was faster, however, and my eyes shot open just in time to see the two men being thrown violently away from Patrick, right into the third, unconscious lackey.

Get 'em, cousin!

"Ah!" the man in the gloves said, looking more excited than worried. "She's developing quickly."

The calm clarity returned as all three men began to rise, picking up their fallen knives, and began to rush at Patrick. I tugged once more and the imaginary door to my magic swung open, revealing a huge, glorious well of energy, swelling, stretching toward me. I reached for it and yanked it out like a loose tooth, letting it free on the world around me, my intentions clear.

Protect Patrick, Zoe, and Mee-maw. Defeat the men attacking them.

A bolt of purplish lightning split the sky, followed by a crash of thunder as the wind picked up into a cylinder that grew tighter, stronger, into a mini-tornado that made a beeline for the melee. I held up both hands, controlling it, bending it to my will. The masked men screamed as they were swept up in the funnel and spun, before being flung in opposite directions, yards apart. I wheeled around, flicking my wrist toward the man in the black gloves, satisfaction bubbling through me as the storm changed course, tearing over the landscape toward him.

Patrick, Zoe, and Mee-maw stood, watching in awe, untouched by the hungry storm.

I swayed on my feet, vision flickering as the tornado closed in on its final target, sending him crashing into the side of Zoe's mausoleum.

Then, I dropped to the ground in a heap of exhaustion.

CHAPTER 12

"Retreat!"

The word was shouted a dozen times, but I couldn't process its meaning through the ringing in my ears.

"What the hell was that?" a second, furious voice demanded a moment before the rumbling of a car's engine sounded. The light that had flooded the cemetery faded, and gravel crunched a moment before the world around us went silent.

It wasn't long before I felt warm hands pulling me to my feet from where I'd been lying on the cold ground.

"They're gone. God, Cricket, are you okay?" Zoe asked, arm still around me for support.

"Not really," I said, the words slurring, though my sense of balance was returning and the ringing in my ears was gradually getting better.

"That was amazing!" Trudy called, sprinting up to us, dim lantern in hand.

"Good work, kiddo," Mee-maw muttered, shaking her head in awe. "That whole tornado thing was pretty slick."

"Thanks," I said, too exhausted to feel more than relief.

"Patrick?"

He stood a few feet away, regarding me, head cocked. His lip had been split, and blood trickled from his nose, but there'd be plenty of time to worry about that later.

He was alive. We all were.

"I'm fine, but we need to get out of here, they probably already called for reinforcements." He hobbled over, turning toward the parking lot as if to hide how cut up his face was.

"What're we going to do about...those?" Trudy asked, pointing to the three mausoleums sticking out of the ground.

I felt a sinking feeling in my stomach but I knew that, regardless of my bone-deep exhaustion, it was up to me to put them back underground.

Who knew what kind of information the Organization could get their hands on if we left them out of the ground?

"Hold me steady," I said, backing further into Zoe as I brought my mind back to the magic I had inside me. I thought it'd take some time to focus again but, when it came to these tombs, my body knew what to do. I pushed down with the few wispy shreds of power I had left and the tombs went down almost instantly.

"You good?" Patrick asked. "I can carry you if you need."

"I'm fine," I said with a weak smile. I pulled away from Zoe and gave walking a try. I stumbled a little at first but got my balance back after just a few steps.

Mee-maw clicked her tongue in approval, patting me on the back a little too hard. "You done good, now let's get you out of here."

"Let's get back to my car," Trudy said, striding quickly past us, a serious look on her face. "I'll get you guys to the bakery."

"What if they follow you?" I started, cutting off at a sharp look from Trudy.

"And you'd rather walk home instead? You'd collapse before

you made it three blocks, not to mention how fast the Organization would find you. We're taking my car."

I nodded slowly, feeling guilty for bringing yet another person into my mess, but knowing that it was the best course of action. "Thank you, Trudy."

She nodded curtly, increasing her pace even more. "Let's keep moving, the Organization could be back any moment now."

Trudy's soccer mom-style minivan was only a few minutes' walk away, parked on the exact opposite side of the cemetery parking lot, and there was hardly another word spoken by the time we made it there, though I noticed that everyone was looking at me like I had two heads while we walked.

"So," Zoe said, breaking the silence as we buckled our seat belts, "I guess that means your powers are back."

I nodded, as elated as I could be, given the circumstances. "Seems like it. I've never done anything like that before, though. I had no idea I had access to so much magic."

I could hardly wait to get back to Maude. As I thought of her, a deep sense of rightness flowed through me. Our connection pulsed and stretched, fat and rich, gilded in a golden light.

"Whether it was the chant, or the burial grounds reawakening my magic, Maude and I are good."

"Excellent," Zoe said with a satisfied nod.

"And how about you, Zoe?" I said, peering over my shoulder at my cousin. "That blast was amazing."

"It felt so good," she said, her mouth splitting into a grin. "I can't believe I pulled it off. It was no tornado, but still..."

"Yeah, that was some display back there, Cricket. Do you think you could replicate it?" Trudy said, not taking her eyes off of the road as she turned onto the main road with a level of caution that seemed a bit over the top, given the situation.

"I'm not sure," I said slowly, considering it. "I couldn't access the magic, at first, but they seemed like they were about to kill Patrick and the door just...opened."

"Maybe you should get almost killed more often," Mee-maw said, an audible smack reverberating through the car as she slapped him on the back. "We could just storm in and blast the whole Organization to smithereens if things get bad enough for you."

Patrick let out a pained chuckle.

"It'd go worse than you think if they were ready for us and had their own magic at their disposal," I said, shivering as I thought about the terrible, incapacitating pain I'd felt on the night I'd lost my connection to Maude and almost died. "We don't even know the full extent of their items."

"Eh, I guess you're right," Mee-maw said grudgingly.

Patrick addressed Mee-maw. "I still think the best plan is to find your magical item before we face off again, if we can help it. They're clearly afraid of battling three witches at once, and I think we should trust them on that."

I nodded to myself. "But we still don't have any leads on that front."

"I wish that old lady just kept the damn thing in her shop," Mee-maw grumbled. "If she had, I'd be witching away like you two by now."

"Tell me about the mausoleums," Patrick said. "Any clues there?"

"Mine was incredible," Zoe began, "there was all kinds of beautiful art and decorations, with books and vials spread all over. At the very back, though, there was this altar with a flower on it and, behind it, there was a box with this strange compass in it." She passed the compass forward, letting Mee-maw and Patrick examine it first.

"I got one kind of like it," Mee-maw said with a chuckle,

"but it's a lot fancier than this old lump of metal." She pulled out hers and handed both to me.

Zoe's was jet black, like mine, but even more matte, and also much heavier. Mee-maw's, on the other hand, was delicate and expensive-looking, with a gold exterior and a fine, thin needle inside. I began to pull my own out to show them, but stopped, blinking as I noticed that the two compasses on my lap were pointing in nearly opposite directions. "That's weird..."

"What is?" Trudy said excitedly, sparing a quick glance before looking back to the road.

"They aren't pointing the same way, like one of them is off or something," I said, pulling my own out to see that it was pointing the same way as Zoe's.

"Let me see," Mee-maw said, reaching forward.

I handed her all three, turning around to see her reaction as she stared at them, her brow furrowed. I cringed as she flicked the side of it a few times, but nothing changed. "Damn thing must be busted," she said. "A shame it wasn't one of those dumpy ones that you two got. Those work good, I bet."

Patrick leaned over to peer down. "Actually, a broken or demagnetized compass would shimmy or spin if you flicked it like that," Patrick said, pointing out the window. "Yours is just pointing a different way. And if Cricket and Zoe's compasses are pointing toward the bakery..." He trailed off as Zoe piped in.

"They must be pointing toward our magical items!"

Despite my exhaustion, I nearly melted with relief at the thought. "That would be a huge break for us."

"That's got to be it! What else would your ancestors want to lead you to so much that they would go through all of this? Mee-maw's compass is pointing almost straight south, and I guarantee it will take us where we need to go," Trudy said as we pulled up to a stop sign, her face lit up with excitement even as she looked cautiously both ways.

A part of me wished we could follow it right now, but we were all at the end of our ropes. We needed rest.

"Just drop us off in front of the alley behind the bakery," Zoe said. "We'll have to sneak in the same way we got out in case the cop is out there. Just take your next left."

Trudy dropped us off on the sidewalk near the back of the bakery several minutes later and we said our goodbyes, though she clearly wanted to stay with us.

"Are you sure it makes sense to leave her to drive home alone?" Zoe asked, whispering as she led the way, though Trudy had already pulled away.

"Her car wasn't parked in the lot, so they didn't see it, and she was in the mausoleum when they attacked," I said. "If they're looking for us, it won't be in Trudy's minivan."

Patrick nodded, trudging along at the back of the group with a slight limp. "Father isn't the type to involve non-magics if he can help it. He's not big on collateral damage. Raises too many questions."

I nodded, but something told me he might still not really grasp the scope of what his father would or wouldn't do if pushed hard enough.

We were all silent as we headed toward the small window on the building closest to us. It would lead us directly into the basement, where Patrick had unboarded the window Connie had snuck through, in order to let us out just an hour or two earlier.

Zoe moved quickly, sliding it open with just the friction of her hands against the glass before hopping in, helping Mee-maw through the long drop once she was inside.

My heart fluttered as I saw a faint light coming toward the alleyway, about twenty feet behind us.

"The bakery is just ahead," a familiar voice was saying. "If they're not there, we'll try the old lady's house."

"Get in," I spat, pushing Patrick forward, but he wouldn't budge.

"You first," he demanded, shaking his head and turning toward the voices.

I opened my mouth to argue but there'd be plenty of time to talk about the silly chivalrous display later, once we were both safe. I rushed forward, shimmying through the open window. Then, I dropped down, inside, gesturing frantically for Patrick to do the same. "Come on!" I hissed, trying not to sound as panicked as I felt.

He grimaced, turning around and sliding his legs inside. He let out a pained groan as he slid through, it was a much tighter squeeze for him than it'd been for the rest of us. We yanked his legs, pulling him through the hole in one shot, making a satisfying sound as he popped through the hole.

He dropped to the ground in a heap, grunting.

I reached to the side quickly, grabbing the wooden board we'd taken off when we'd snuck out to go to the graveyard earlier, before looking up just in time to see the bright light sweeping down the backside of the strip mall and moving steadily toward us. I lifted the piece of wood in front of the window as quickly as possible and held it in place as I gasped for air.

For long minutes, none of us moved or spoke. Soon enough, though, it became clear that we hadn't been spotted. They would know soon enough, if they didn't already, that we were hiding out in the bakery. But we were banking on the cop out front and the location on a relatively busy street to keep them from pushing a full-on confrontation here. Tonight wasn't the night to test our theory. Not as beat as we all were.

Not if the voice I heard belonged to the man I thought it did.

I barely repressed a shudder as I pushed the memories away.

"Talk about cutting it close," Mee-maw murmured.

I wanted to reply, but I couldn't find the words. I just leaned forward and pressed my head against the wooden slab, trying not to burst into relieved tears.

We'd made it through another harrowing experience, by the skin of our teeth. One more battle, down. But if we were going to win this war, we needed to get one step ahead of these guys.

And we needed to do it fast.

CHAPTER 13

"That was him," I muttered a short while later. "I'm almost sure of it."

We'd finally decided to risk the noise of hammering the board in again, and Zoe was busy at the task as the rest of us took a breath.

"Who?" she asked, pausing to look back at me.

"The man with the necklace." The memory of being tortured came back in a flood, and I swallowed back a rush of bile.

"It's okay," Patrick muttered, reaching out to give my shoulder a comforting squeeze. "Even if they wind up realizing we're here, he's not going to risk breaking in tonight."

"You think we should go back out there and blast him?" Mee-maw asked, her already wrinkled face getting even more wrinkled as she frowned.

"Definitely not," I managed through my bone-dry throat. "He is fresh as a daisy and ready to fight. We're all feeling like crap on the bottom of a shoe. I don't even know if I have anything to blast him with. But his presence means they definitely called in reinforcements."

Once the board was back in place, the four of us trudged up the steps to the bakery and filed into the kitchen.

"I don't know about you guys, but I haven't showered since we left Greg's. I'm going to set up a makeshift bathing area over there." Zoe pointed to the industrial dishwasher and sprayer in the corner of the room. "Then, I'm going to crank the water up to scalding and work these tired muscles over a little."

Mee-maw's face lit up. "Oooh, lemme get my purse! I've got some trial-sized shampoo bottles that I stole from that hotel last time I went to visit my cousin Doris in Saskatchewan."

"Mee-maw...cousin Doris died, like, ten years ago."

"Yeah, I've been keeping them in there since then because I knew they'd come in handy. And I was right!"

"You sure were," Zoe agreed. "Let's get some clean clothes out of the Walmart bags for each of us, Mee-maw. I've got loads of dish towels to dry off with. Might take a few, but they'll do in a pinch. I'll get you all set up for your shower, first, and while you clean up, I'll make a little nightcap. I've got some Kahlua in the kitchen that I usually save for my Mexican hot chocolate cupcakes that's got my name written all over it. A nice Kahlua and cream, followed by a hot shower before I hit the sleeping bag sounds like heaven."

"If you're buying, make mine a double, hold the cream," Mee-maw grumbled, pressing a hand to her lower back with a wince.

"You'll have what I'm having, and a weak one at that. The doctor doesn't want you drinking much." Zoe scrubbed a hand over her weary face and shot me a glance. "Unless you think we should just take a nap and then head right back out tonight and find Mee-maw's item?"

Everyone was spent, no doubt about it. We needed to regroup and recharge before we could continue, Mee-maw more than the rest of us.

I shook my head. "Nope. Let's stick to the plan. After what just happened, we need to lay low anyway. They know that we got something important from the cemetery and they know my magic is strong now. They're still patrolling, even now, looking for us. We'll wait until tomorrow, at least, before making another move."

"Are you sure?" Mee-maw asked, her gazing locking with mine. "If we have to go, we go. I might be old, but I'm tough. I won't have you coddling me."

"Nope," I assured her. "It's just too dangerous. I wouldn't do it whether you were with us or not."

Patrick remained suspiciously silent and, despite his assurances on the way back to the bakery, I had to wonder if he was hurting more than he was letting on.

"Let's get us the stuff for that shower and drink then, Zoe. I'm about to find my magical item, I want to celebrate," Mee-maw said, the excitement evident in her voice in spite of her exhaustion.

"We'll take a turn after you guys. I want to check on Maude," I said.

Patrick trailed after me into the back office, but I could hear Mee-maw chattering away as we went.

"You think it might be a broom? Under normal circumstances, I'm not a fan of brooms, but I've always wanted to fly. Oh! Or what if it's a wand? That would be cool."

Her voice faded as I closed the door behind us and turned to face Patrick.

"You think she's okay?" I asked him softly.

"I think that you were right to put off the hunt for her item until tomorrow, for sure," he said, propping his bottom against the table and leaning back. "But I don't think we should push it much beyond that. Remember, once she has the item, she'll be able to heal more quickly, and generally feel more energized. At her age, the sooner she connects with it, the better."

I processed those words, realizing with a start that he was right. Even with my limited connection to Maude at that point, I still hadn't felt a twinge from my few-day-old knife wound all night. And, heck, before a few weeks ago, I'd have typically been sore from sitting on a chair too long, never mind sleeping on the floor of the library. While it hadn't been comfortable in the least, I could honestly say that my back hadn't ached at all.

"Agree," I said, gesturing to his torso. "Now, spill it. How bad is it?"

"It's fine."

Only then did I realize that there was a dark stain spreading on his navy-colored shirt.

"Dang it, Patrick. Why are you trying to be macho right now? Same with making me go in through the window first. That's got to stop," I muttered as I charged toward him. "Once Mee-maw gets her item, you'll literally be the only one among us without the ability to heal quickly. Zoe doesn't have a handle on her potions-making yet, and if something happens to you--" I broke off as I lifted the hem of his shirt carefully away from the wound.

"If something happens to me, what?" he asked, his voice husky.

I swallowed hard and pulled away. "We will lose a valuable informant," I finished lamely.

I busied myself rifling through Zoe's desk, in search of the first aid kit, but I could feel the weight of his stare.

"Is that all I am to you, then?"

Was that hurt in his voice? He had a lot of nerve, considering he'd almost gotten me killed.

But deep inside, I knew that was just a defense mechanism kicking up. He'd proven himself time and time again since that fateful night. I think I was just terrified that, without a wedge between us, forcing us apart, we'd come crashing together, on a collision course that would lead me straight to Heartbreak City.

"You're a friend, as well," I conceded, clearing my throat as I turned, first aid kit in hand. "Which is why you're going to humor me and have a seat while I clean you up, yes?"

His gaze grew hooded as he studied me for a long moment before unfolding his long, lean body into the closest of the two office chairs.

"Fine. Have at it, Florence."

I opened the little, white box and rummaged through until I found some gauze pads and peroxide, along with a little pile of bandages.

If I was being honest with myself, I'd have to admit that it was good to have a task to focus on. My brain kept trying to rewind the tape back to that voice...that necklace. The instrument of horror and agony I would give almost anything to forget.

I shoved the thought back again and instructed Patrick to unbutton his shirt.

The command sent his mouth kicking up into the crooked half-smile that had surely launched a thousand skirts.

"Not even going to take me out to dinner first, eh?" he teased, even as he made quick work of the buttons.

Any hopes of a witty retort died on my lips as the two sides of the shirt fell open to reveal his muscular chest and abs.

Luckily, my daze only lasted a moment as my gaze zeroed in on his injury.

"Just a scratch?" I asked, reaching for the gauze and peroxide. "That's pretty deep, and there's a scrape right beneath it."

"My struggle through the window sort of compounded the issue. Still, though, I think it looks worse than it is."

I sure hoped so, because as much as I appreciated him sewing me up a few days before, I wasn't confident I could return the favor without passing out.

After soaking one of the pads and bending my head closer, I gently began to wipe the blood away. Because I was standing and he was seated, all I had to do was lift my head a fraction and we'd be eye to eye.

"Cricket?"

"Hmm?" I murmured, refusing to look up.

"Do you ever wonder what would've happened if we met at a different time? A different place."

My throat went tight and I continued to dab, even though I'd gotten most of the blood cleaned away. He'd been right. The cut was ugly and long, and the scrape made it look even worse, but it wasn't very deep. Nothing a few butterfly bandages couldn't handle. I was pretty sure, of the two of us, I was in a lot more discomfort than he was at the moment.

"Umm...yeah. I mean, I don't know," I hedged, backing away to admire my handiwork.

"Well, I do," he said, reaching out to cup my jaw. "I wonder all the time. And I can't help but hope that the universe designed it so that we would meet, one way or another, because we have a destiny to fulfill."

I was powerless to stop myself from meeting his gaze now, and my busy hands fell to my sides.

"Our priority is to bring your coven back to its former strength and take down the Organization," he murmured as his fingers slid to my nape. "But know this. The second it's done...the second we win this war, my next priority is to get you into my bed and keep you there for as long as you'll let me."

If I'd wondered about his intentions since finding out who he truly was, I wondered no more.

My tongue stuck to the roof of my mouth as he drew me closer, until we were nose to nose.

"I like you, Cricket. I like everything about you. Your laugh. Your wisecrack remarks. The way you protect those you love and fight for what's right. And I'm finding it damn hard to resist that mouth of yours, even now, in the midst of the direst of circumstances. Can I kiss you?"

My knees knocked together once before my head bobbed up and down of its own accord.

"Thank God."

His lips touched mine in the softest of kisses. An almost reverent exploration that stole my breath. I leaned into him on a groan as he gently nipped my bottom lip with his teeth and then tugged, before tracing the spot with his tongue.

I swayed, clutching his broad shoulders for support as his free arm stole around my bottom.

"I was going to ask if you guys wanted a midnight snack, but it seems like you've got your hands full, so I'll just sneak on out of here…"

I could hear the chuckle in Zoe's voice as I jerked away from Patrick with a start.

This was what happened when you were hiding out from a cult with family. Zero expectation of privacy.

"Don't let me stop you," Zoe continued. "I just needed to grab the bags with our clothes and I'll get out of your hair."

True to her word, she melted out of the room a minute later, but the spell had been broken. Now, all I felt was awkward and self-conscious.

"Look, Patrick, I liked you…"

He drew back like I'd stricken him and I rushed to continue.

"I *still* like you. But I can't make any decisions about anything except right now. I need every ounce of my concentration just to figure out what I'm supposed to do, and how not to botch this all up and get my cousin and grandmother killed in the process. They're looking to me to lead them," I said with an almost hysterical laugh. "Me. I have no clue what I'm doing, and everything is happening so fast."

Patrick stood and took my hand, giving it a reassuring squeeze. "I'm not asking for promises, or even an answer. I wasn't honest with you about my intentions when we first met, so I wanted to be honest about them now. I want you. It's a declaration, not a question. If and when you want to do something about it, you let me know. I'll be here...ready, and waiting."

The words sent a shudder through me, leaving me breathless, so I just nodded.

"Thanks for playing nurse. I'm going to go see if I can help them set up the hosing off station, yeah? Why don't you go ahead and see Maude?"

Grateful for the reprieve, I nodded and Patrick headed out of the room. I sucked in a stabilizing breath and scurried over to the closet where we'd hidden Maude before we left. I couldn't wait to see her after all this. There was little chance anyone would've taken her with the cop right outside, even if they'd known where she was, but unlike before, I wasn't sure if she was taken if she'd find her way back to me as she had so many times. We decided we couldn't be too careful, and had buried her under a pile of old flour sacks.

I sat down on the rug and unearthed her in a rush, tossing the sacks aside. And as much as my interaction with Patrick had sent me for a tailspin, the second I saw the old girl, everything felt right with the world.

"Maude," I whispered, reaching out to stroke the keys lovingly. They felt electric...alive.

Perfect. Our bond was stronger than ever, the knowledge

filled me with joy and gratitude. Whatever else needed doing, I knew we could manage it, together.

I sat there for a long time, just letting those good feelings replenish my soul, but the need to type never came. Maybe even Maude sensed that I'd maxed out mentally for the day—but I knew in my bones, when the time was right, she would let me know.

A while later, I lifted her from her hiding spot, onto the desk, and headed back out to join the others.

Patrick sat on a chair in the storefront of the bakery with a steaming mug in hand, his hair damp and curling at the edges. Zoe's makeshift shower situation must've worked well enough, because he looked clean as a whistle and more relaxed than I'd seen him since...well, before I knew he wasn't just a handyman.

"I don't know about you guys, but I felt kind of like an elephant at the zoo," Mee-maw was saying with a throaty chuckle. "Pretty handy, the way the kitchen floor has the drain in it and all."

"By the way, don't think I'm not telling Cricket that you spent at *least* twenty minutes under the hot spray," Zoe teased.

"I'm not the one paying the bill," Mee-maw, a shower dictator in her own house, crowed, pausing to take a long pull from her glass.

"Did you leave any hot water for me?" I teased, stepping into the room.

All eyes flicked my way, and I was happy to see that my cousin and grandmother looked much better than when I'd seen them last. Apparently, all it took was a win and some soap and water to breathe new life into a cause.

"How about a drink, first?" Zoe asked.

I nodded and accepted the glass she had all ready for me with a nod of thanks.

"Trudy texted, by the way. She got home safe, no problem," Mee-maw said.

"All in all, a really good day."

There were nods all around, but no more words. We sat in companionable silence for a half an hour, each lost in our own thoughts as we unwound. When Mee-maw's head began to bob, Patrick offered to set up the futon mats with our sleeping bags on top of them. Zoe poured herself another nightcap as I headed for my much-needed elephant shower.

I had to admit, it wasn't perfect, but the hot water felt amazing, and lulled me into a warm cocoon of relaxation. By the time I climbed into my sleeping bag a while later, it was nearly three AM and I was so tired that I didn't even have the energy to feel nervous that Patrick lay just a few feet away. I could barely even figure out how to unzip my bag, never mind contemplate seduction.

My head had barely hit the pillow when my eyes drifted shut and the darkness drew me under.

CHAPTER 14

THE BURNING WAS DEEP. *So hot, it almost felt cold...at first. Then, it was pure agony.*

"Burn, witch, burn!"

I barely registered the chant of the raging mob that had gathered to watch the show, though. The skin on the bottom of my feet had started to sizzle, bubble and pop.

A primal scream tore from my throat as I tried in vain to escape my shackles, to no avail.

"Let the heretics burn for their crimes!"

The flames licked at my ankles as I tried to think past the pain to find my magic—that tiny, glowing ember within me—and bring it to life, but a second scream broke my concentration.

I looked up to see a second woman tied to a post just yards away, kicking...snarling, scratching to get away, with everything she had. Beaten and bruised, she was no match for the men locking her in place, dangling her above a pile of dried brush, kindling and logs.

"Another! Another!" the crowd chanted.

"No!" I howled, over and over until my throat was raw. Just as one of her captors lifted a torch to set her pyre aflame, I tried

one last time. A deep dive for my magic through the terror and pain, grabbing onto and holding tight.

"No!" I shouted one last time. The flames that had engulfed my legs died, even as the nearby torch flickered and went out, in a puff of smoke.

The shouts of bloodthirsty glee and the catcalls went silent as a fearful murmur rolled through the crowd.

There was no time to waste. I sucked in a breath, ready to send out another wave that would hopefully free us.

"Not so fast, little witch."

The voice sent pure dread running through me and I turned to see who had spoken.

I would recognize that scruffy beard and those cold eyes anywhere. But far scarier than his face was the necklace around his throat. A gold chain with a small crystal amulet dangling from it. Such a pretty, elegant thing.

Who'd have known by looking at that, it was an instrument of unimaginable torture?

Just the thought of it had me frozen in terror for a moment. And a moment was all it took.

"Gotcha," he whispered, closing his grubby fist around the amulet and squeezing.

This time, when I started screaming, I didn't stop.

"Cricket? Damn it, Cricket, wake up."

I gasped and bolted upright, frantically straining to see.

"Where am I?"

"Shh, it's okay," a low masculine voice murmured. "You're in the bakery with me."

I sucked in a shuddering breath and tried to slow the pitiful pounding of my heart as the vague shadow of a man's face came into view in the dark room.

Patrick.

Not at all in the clutches of the prison guard who had oh-so-casually tortured me.

God, it had felt so real.

My eyes stung with unshed tears and I bent my legs at the knees and pressed my forehead against them.

Patrick's big, warm hand moved in soothing circles on my back, but he stayed silent. The only sound in the room was that of Mee-maw snoring in the far corner.

Maybe it was hearing the bastard's voice that had set off the horrible nightmares. Maybe it had been reconnecting with my ancestors and imagining what they'd suffered. Maybe it was a little of both. Whatever the case, I was left feeling raw and broken.

"Want to talk about it?"

I shook my head but didn't lift it.

"Was it about the necklace guy?"

I nodded.

"He'll pay for what he did to you, Cricket. So will my father. I won't rest until I see that happen. And, honestly, I don't know if I can ever forgive myself for my part in putting you in that situation." I already knew how much he regretted his actions. Still, it was nice to hear the words again, and the warm, smooth baritone was comforting.

"I don't blame you. Not anymore, at least," I said softly as I lifted my head and faced him in the dim light. "I was mad, at first. Like, really, really mad. Now, I feel like I've seen enough of your character to believe that you must've had your reasons."

The silence stretched between us for long enough that I started to wonder if he'd even heard me.

"I thought so. But now I'm not so sure." I could sense the tension in his body, pressed against my side as he continued. "Cricket...My mother is a witch."

It took a second to process what he'd said, but once I did, my mouth swung open in shock.

"Are you kidding me? Why would your father be so..."

The words died on my lips as my brain shot back to the day we'd met, just a few short weeks ago, despite it feeling like years. I'd complimented him at the bar over drinks...told him his mama must've raised him right, and he'd said--

"Wait. She is a witch, or was one? You told me your mother was dead."

"That was part of the cover I was given by the Organization, along with the backstory about my sister living in the U.S.," he admitted with a wince. "I'm an only child."

"But I looked it up online when I started getting suspicious of you..." I trailed off as he shook his head, eyes full of apology.

"The Organization ensures that our covers are able to withstand pretty heavy scrutiny. I'm sorry, Cricket."

I searched for some outrage, but I'd known that his persona was a lie before I'd chosen to trust him again. The semantics at this point didn't really matter. "What's done is done. I want to hear about your Mom, Patrick. What happened to her?" I asked, and gestured for him to keep talking.

He looked away and nodded. "Great question. The story I'd been told my whole life was that my mother left us. That the mom I knew—the one who had come to all my ball games, bandaged my knees when I skinned them, used to play hide and seek with me—found out she had magic on her forty-fifth birthday and left because the magic and her evil, mind-twisted coven had convinced her that they mattered more than our family. I believed him because things had been strange at home for months. She was a chronic mix of exhausted and elated as she tried to figure out how to tap into her powers. Suddenly, it was all she had time for anymore. A few months later, I came home from school and she was gone. Clothes, suitcases and all. I had no reason to doubt my father's version of things until recently. Hell, she'd even left me a keepsake and a letter letting me know she'd reconnected with her coven and needed to explore her powers before she could come home. That was thirty-three years ago. I was ten."

My gut churned at the bitter sadness in his voice and I laced my fingers with his, giving them a squeeze as he continued.

"As days turned into months, and then years, I just accepted my father's view of things as the truth. He got involved with the Organization after a while. At first, I thought it was so he could find her. Convince her to come back. But as I got older, I realized he was harboring an impotent sort of fury that he aimed at magic in general. He viewed it as the root of so much evil and grief. For years, he didn't involve me, but after I graduated college, he asked me to join. I was missing her so much, then. I still felt so lost in the world without her, and would've given anything to see her again. Show her the man I'd become. See if she was proud of me."

Tears flowed freely down my face now as he laid his soul bare.

"I told my father I would join him to help rid the world of magic, but at the time, all I wanted was their resources to help me find my mom. In the twenty years since, the Organization has located twelve covens around the world, but none of them was my mother's. Up until we found you guys and they called in all hands on deck, I was part-time only, mainly involved in logistics. Getting teams to various locations, ensuring funds and passports were in order, smoothing over red tape...back end stuff. The rest of the time, I was searching the globe for my mother. Now, I can't help but feel sick at the thought of what would happen if I'd found her. Would he have done the same to her as he's done to you? Did she leave because she didn't love me enough to stay, like my father said, or because she knew if she stayed, she and her coven would've been slaughtered like cattle by the men my father now calls brothers in arms."

I couldn't help but imagine Patrick as a young boy—skinned knees, dark curls, wounded eyes, waiting by the door for his mother to come back—and it was killing me.

"The worst part of it? Is that those twelve other covens are almost certainly gone now. My father and his men murdered them, and stole their very essence. Those lines snuffed out. Those witches leaving behind sons and daughters, too. No more. Not my mother's coven, and not yours. We have to stop him, Cricket. Whatever it takes, we have to stop him."

I pressed my forehead against his shoulder and felt a hot tear plop on my cheek, mixing with my own.

"We will, Patrick. I promise."

I had no business making a promise like that. Hell, there was a fifty-fifty shot I'd be dead before the week was over. But until then, I was casting my lot with Patrick and my coven.

And we were going to find a way to win this war, or die trying.

CHAPTER 15

"Something wrong, Zoe?" Mee-maw asked from her place at the head of the table. We were all assembled in the back room for a later breakfast of black coffee, French toast, maple syrup, and fresh strawberries. Not a bad way to start the day, even if we were on the run from people who wanted us dead.

Zoe, who had been staring into her coffee mug as if in a trance, aimlessly stirring it with one finger, dragged her gaze up to my grandmother and stared at her for a long moment. "Not really," she replied.

"Those bags under your eyes tell a different story," Mee-maw retorted as she glanced down at the compass in her hand for the millionth time, before turning her attention back to Zoe. "You mustn't have slept a wink. They're about the size of Alaska!"

"Gee, thanks," Zoe muttered. "I'm so glad I have you here to point that out for me, Mee-maw. It's almost enough to make me try for another batch of cinnamon buns."

"Hey, you're not the only one," Mee-maw replied defensively, holding up her hands. "My lower back has been killing me, and I don't even have a big macho man to massage the pain away." She gave Patrick a pointed glance, one of her eyebrows cocking up just a little. "Not that I'd be complaining if I did," she added.

"Mee-maw!" I exclaimed, feeling my cheeks heating up as I took a sip from my own coffee cup.

"I'm just saying--"

"You know what, new subject," Zoe interrupted, straightening up in her chair. "We need to figure out what to do about your item, Mee-maw."

As I studied my cousin, I couldn't help but note that our grandmother was right. Zoe was looking even rougher than the rest of us, and something told me she hadn't slept much.

I shot a glance to Patrick, and squirmed as I caught him staring at me.

Last night had been...interesting. I wasn't about to pretend it wasn't a little weird waking up next to the guy, especially after the intimate talk we'd had. I wasn't used to sharing so much with someone I'd known for such a short time, but nothing about our situation was normal right now.

Besides, there was something about him that I couldn't put my finger on, something that set me at ease. I felt it from that first drink we'd had together, but last night's conversation had just driven it home. And now I felt like I understood him better, trusted him even more. Who knew? Maybe, when this was all over, if we lived to tell the tale...

But that was a big if, and those kinds of plans were best left for later.

"I say we just go walk out in a group, guns blazing, follow the compass, and take the darn thing," Mee-maw suggested, holding the sleek, golden device high. "They know what you two can do, now. If anyone's watching the bakery and they don't run for the hills the second you start summoning a storm, it's their own fault."

"Guns blazing?" Zoe asked incredulously, crossing her arms. "In broad daylight? Be reasonable. We only have one gun and a bunch of knives, and none of us are going to go around town shooting, calling attention to ourselves and potentially involving anyone else."

"Look," Patrick spoke up, crumpling up his napkin and setting it aside, "as much as we need that item, I'm not sure it would be such a good idea to just charge out there. These people are strategists, and they've been doing this a very long time. They're going to be waiting for us to make a mistake, and you can believe me when I say that if we act rashly, they're going to take full advantage." He stretched his arms back for a moment, wincing at the movement.

I couldn't help leaning in and putting a hand on his shoulder. "Are you okay?" I asked. "How's your chest?"

Mee-maw snorted at that. "You'd know better than he would, Cricket. You had your face buried in it when I woke up this morning."

I swallowed hard, feeling my ears start to burn as Mee-maw cackled at her own joke. Even Zoe shot me a grin, winking as she looked from me to Patrick.

He gave me a warm smile, slipping my hand off his shoulder and squeezing it gently. "I'll survive," he told me. "You did a good job dressing the wound."

"It was the least I could do," I replied quietly, meeting his eyes for a moment, and for a few seconds, none of us spoke.

Mee-maw was the one who finally broke the silence. "Enough of Bogey and Bacall, here. Back to business. Let's hear it, smarty-pants," she said, rounding on Zoe, "what do you suggest? The sooner we find my item, the better, and I say the longer we wait, the longer we risk the Organization getting their grubby little paws on it and keeping it from me until they catch you two."

"You're not wrong," I conceded, pushing my plate away and propping my elbows up on the table. "Sooner or later, we are going to need to make a trip out of the bakery to follow the compass. The key is doing it without attracting the Organization's attention and being followed."

"Not to mention, the cop's," Zoe added. "I saw the guy they had posted last night. He was doing his job, I'll give him that. They seemed skeptical already. We can't have them see us sneaking around and give them another reason to think we're up to something. And I don't know about you, but I think we've all had our share of climbing out that stupid window."

I groaned. "I didn't even think about that."

Zoe opened her mouth to say something else, but Patrick spoke up before she could. "A distraction, maybe? Depending on how many people they have on us, we could split up."

"Didn't we already discuss this? Have you ever watched a horror movie?" Mee-maw demanded. "That's about the last thing we should do."

"I'm open to other suggestions," Patrick replied, sighing and running a hand through his hair.

"I might have something," Zoe said, and we all turned to her.

"Well, don't leave us in suspense," Mee-maw told her. "Let's hear it!"

"Here's the thing," Zoe began, but she was interrupted by the sound of a tapping on the bakery door. The four of us all looked at each other before Patrick got to his feet, the half-finished French toast momentarily forgotten. I couldn't help but feel a pang of unease as he crept to the window to take a peek outside, tensing up in anticipation of a gunshot or a scream. They wouldn't be so bold as to come knocking on the front door, would they?

Instead, Patrick turned back to us, lowering the curtain, and announced, "It's one of the cops from yesterday."

He was right; as we filed out of the back room and into the shop area, I could make out the lanky form of Deputy Rasmusson, his arms crossed over his chest and a look on his face that said he was fit to be tied. Zoe cleared her throat and unlocked the door, allowing him to enter.

"Morning," he said flatly, putting a hand on his utility belt as he sized up the four of us. "How is everyone today?" He didn't sound the slightest bit interested, and his tone was cold—ice cold, actually.

My stomach sank. Whatever this was, it couldn't be good.

"We're all right, all things considered," I replied, tucking some stray hair behind my ear. "And yourself?"

"Not great, to be perfectly honest with you," Rasmusson replied.

"Where's Sheriff Webber?" Zoe asked, although whether out of professional or personal interest, I couldn't rightly say.

"Sheriff Webber is back at the station, working on cases that are actually urgent," Rasmusson replied, steering his pinched gaze to her. "He's decided that there are more important uses of his time—and Rocky Knoll tax dollars—than chasing ghosts and following false leads."

"False leads...?" My gut churned. "I'm sorry, Deputy, but what are you--"

"Save the feigned shock, Cricket," Rasmusson interrupted, holding up a hand and turning back to me. "You've done enough damage already. I'm just here to tell you all that we're officially closing your case file, and we won't be investigating your... claims...further. You should be ashamed of yourself. I knew it sounded shady, but you know my wife, and she feels sorry for you, so I gave you the benefit of the doubt."

"I'm sorry?" I asked, anger replacing fear. "Wait a minute,

you can't be saying I made it all up. Why the hell would I lie about something like this?"

"Language, ma'am." Rasmusson sniffed. "I honestly have no idea, and to be honest, I don't care. There was absolutely nothing credible about the statement you gave to us yesterday."

I fumbled for a moment, my mouth opening and closing. "I showed you my wounds. And what about the factory we told you about? Have you even gone to look? It's right where we told you, right?"

"It was," the deputy confirmed, "and it was virtually empty. All cobwebs and collapsing foundations. It looked like it hadn't been used in years, if not decades. There's no way they were using it for some kind of ritual sacrifice less than a week ago."

I could only stare at him, stunned, my mind racing. I knew they'd clean it up, and I'd hoped that alone would be enough to keep the police investigating and hopefully keeping watch over the shop. But to make it look like it hadn't been used in decades? Patrick, Zoe, and Mee-maw had all been there, too; they had seen the gallows, the Organization's supplies. One look at them was enough to tell me they were as shocked as I was.

Clearly, the Organization had used magic of some kind, and it was throwing a real wrench in our plans.

"Listen here, pal," Mee-maw began, jabbing a finger in his direction, "we can back Cricket up on this. We saw what they'd done to that place. Just because they cleaned up after themselves--"

"Dust, an inch thick. Sorry, but you're asking us to believe something that is, quite frankly, impossible," Rasmusson said, cutting her off before returning his gaze to me. "Not to mention that it's awfully convenient for you to claim someone's after you a day before your house burns down."

I gaped at him, my eyes practically bugging out of my skull. "Burned down? What are you talking about?!" I shot a frantic glance in Mee-maw's direction. "Something happened to Mee-maw's house?"

"Not your grandmother's house," replied the deputy. "Yours. The one you shared with your ex, Gregory Hallowell?" He let out a dry chuckle, shaking his head. "And that note was a real stroke of genius, too—making it look like a crazy cult was after you there. 'Surrender, Dorothy.' That's from The Wizard of Oz, right? Honestly, I have to give you credit for trying. Creepy. It's like something out of a horror movie. What we haven't figured out yet was whether you all concocted the story to make it look like someone burned your house down to collect the insurance money, or you set the house on fire to support this cult story because you're all batshit crazy. Trust me, though, we're going to find out."

But I was hardly listening to him. My ears were ringing, adrenaline was surging through my veins, and my heart was pumping so fast I felt like it was on the verge of exploding. Without even thinking about it, I grabbed Patrick by the arm, sagging against him as I ran a hand over my forehead, which had gone cold and clammy.

This was bad. This was very, very bad.

"What about Greg?" I managed to choke out. "When did this happen?"

"The very night you called us with this tall tale," replied Rasmusson. "Your ex-husband is in the hospital right now. Your kids tried getting in touch with you for the past day and a half, but your phone went straight to voicemail. They started to get worried, and that was when they called the Sheriff's office. And thank God they did. We'd still be chasing our tails right now if they hadn't."

I could feel myself growing weak and trembly, a combination of fear and anger the only thing keeping me from collapsing right then and there. The Organization wasn't afraid of leaving a trail of destruction in their wake, and in that moment, I felt helpless to stop it. "My kids," I stammered. "W-were they in the house?"

Deputy Rasmusson's expression softened slightly.

"Your kids are fine, Ms. Hawthorne. Everyone is fine. Apparently, your ex-husband wasn't even inside when it happened. When he pulled up and saw the flames, he ran in to rescue his bowling ball, and that was how he got burned. He'll recover just fine. As for you, though..." His voice went cold again. "We have damn close to enough evidence to bring you in for falsifying a police report already. And you can be sure other charges are to follow."

"You can't be serious!" Mee-maw protested, and I could feel tears welling up in my eyes. "She just lost her house, her ex is in the hospital, and you're trying to arrest her?"

"There are serious charges involved," Rasmusson replied. "The sheriff mentioned arson, insurance fraud..."

"Hang on," Patrick said, stepping forward and holding up a hand, but the deputy just kept going.

"And then come to find out that the warehouse you sent us to couldn't have been the scene of a bloody crime."

"Why would we have sent you there, then?" Patrick persisted. "You have to know that was in good faith. How often do you have three witnesses to a crime? Look, I understand how far-fetched this seems, and I know it doesn't look good for us. But you have to believe us—we're as in the dark about all this as you are, and if you pull out of this now, you're risking other lives. What if these people don't stop? That's going to be blood on your hands. Maybe you went to the wrong factory. There are a few over there."

I could see the deputy's resolve wavering.

"It's possible, I guess..." Rasmusson said, sighing, "Even if we continue the investigation, we still have to pursue the arson angle."

"We get it, believe me," Patrick replied. "Please. Just give it a little more time. If you don't unearth some proof soon, you can shut the whole thing down and do what you have to do."

There was a long, tense silence. I could see Rasmusson struggling to stay aloof and losing the battle—Patrick's way with words was astounding. Finally, he ran a hand through his hair, looking tired.

"All right," he said at last. "We'll keep a guard posted outside for the next few days, unless we find proof that this was all a hoax, of course."

It was a good thing, too, because if the Organization had eyes on the bakery, they'd surely seen us let the deputy in and were aware of our location now.

Rasmusson continued on, his expression stern. "But if that happens, there will be consequences. Not just for you, Cricket, but for all of you."

"Deal," Patrick said without missing a beat, extending a hand to the deputy. "You won't regret it. I promise."

Rasmusson only nodded, muttering to himself as he shuffled back out the door. We watched him go, in a daze, and it was all I could do to slump into a chair.

"This is bad, you guys," Zoe said, putting her head in her hands.

"You're telling me," I replied. "That note..." I lifted my head. It felt like it took all my strength. "They knew we'd been there and when they found we'd gone, they torched the place to show me they could. My kids could've been there. The note was a threat, letting me know that I need to turn myself over to them, or they are willing to go to any lengths. What's next? Mee-maw's house? There's no two ways about it. Whatever hesitance your father may have felt about involving outsiders, he's clearly over it now. Greg could've been killed."

I glanced up at Patrick, whose expression was filled with pain as he nodded sadly.

"Agreed."

"You should call him," Mee-maw suggested quietly. "Check on him, make sure he's doing all right."

"On it. We're going to need to keep tabs on them all, now."

Wordlessly, Zoe went to the back and retrieved the bakery phone, dialing the hospital number and waiting for someone to connect me with Greg. She handed it to me as we waited, her face lined with concern, and I could feel myself breathing heavily as I put it up to my ear.

"Mom?" The familiar voice of my daughter Lizzie came through on the other end. "Mom, are you okay?"

"Honey?" I said, relaxing a little even as I fought the urge to weep. "It's me. Are you all right?"

"I'm fine," she replied. "What about you? What happened? Where are you?"

"I'm at Cousin Zoe's bakery," I explained. "I'm okay. Where's your father? Is he awake?"

"Yeah, he's here." Her tone had gone from worried to chilly in an instant. "He's in a lot of pain, burns all up his arm and hand. What the hell were you doing, leaving your phone off like that this whole time? Dad told me you got hurt on a hike and I was worried sick something went wrong when we couldn't get in touch with you."

"Lizzie," I began, trying to keep my voice level, "I'm sorry. I lost my phone and…it's a long story. Is he there? Can you put him on?"

"He's getting his burns cleaned at the moment," she snapped, and I realized with a sinking feeling that she blamed me for this. Little did she know how right she was. "You should come here and make sure he's okay. The smoke inhalation could've killed him."

"Listen," I pleaded, rubbing at my throbbing temples, "I can't right now. Zoe and I are in the middle of an issue at the bakery and--"

"Are you kidding me? Dad almost died and you can't even be bothered to visit him at the hospital?"

"I will," I protested, "as soon as I can. I just need you guys to be patient. Things are...a little weird right now. Can you tell him I hope he's okay?"

"Tell him yourself, if you ever decide to stop being so selfish," she snapped, and then she hung up the phone.

I stared at the receiver as I let out a long breath. The others were staring at me, concerned and apprehensive. My heart felt like a block of ice in my chest, which was weird, because my blood was boiling as I lifted my chin.

"They thought I was a thorn in their side before?" I muttered, fists clenching as I imagined the hell I planned to rain down on the bastards that had torched my house. "They've gone too far. We're going to find Mee-maw's item, and we're going to find it today. And then?"

I lifted my head and met Patrick's gaze.

"I'm going to remind them why they fear witches."

CHAPTER 16

"I GET that you're upset, and you have every right to be," Patrick said, his voice calm. "But the last thing we need to do is lead the Organization right to your grandmother's item. If they get to it before we do, they can take their time and pick the two of you off the second we let our guard down. The strength is in the full coven."

I turned to him, clenching my fists and holding back a serious urge to punch him as I spoke. "You were the one saying we had to find it ASAP. Now my kids almost lost their father, and you want me to sit around and wait even a second?"

"Going off half-cocked is a bad idea, Cricket. Magic and fury are a bad mix. At least check and see if Maude has anything to say about what to do first."

"I don't need to," I said, with icy determination. "My last prediction right before the cinnamon buns wore off was as clear as it needed to be, if you ask me. 'Time is ticking.' Maude agrees with me. We need to act now. But even if she didn't, we're going to be here without a guard tomorrow, and that's *if* I don't get arrested for arson." On a roll, I turned to Zoe, who looked like she was about to doze off. "And *you,* how can you be half asleep when the Organization just burned my house down?"

She wiped her eyes as she stood up, walking toward the kitchen. "Well...as I was about to say before I was so rudely interrupted by that police officer, I was up basically all night coming up with something that I think might make it a lot safer to look for Mee-maw's item."

"What do you mean?" I asked quickly, the guilt at snapping at her hardly registering past the overwhelming sense of urgency and terror that I felt pushing me to find Mee-maw's item and finish our battle with the Organization once and for all.

"Banana nut muffins," she said, grinning as she pulled a tray of muffins out of the oven, which had been turned off. "With a drizzle of invisibility icing."

"Invisibility? Sweet!" Mee-maw exclaimed.

"Have you tested them?" I asked, striding toward her.

"Yeah," she said, "but not this batch, and it's hard to tell how well they're actually working because you can still see yourself after you eat them. There are some...other effects and I've been operating under the assumption that the invisibility is getting stronger as those increase, though we won't know for sure until we try. These ones were my most recent batch and I was asleep by the time they were finished cooking. Thank god for the "timed bake" button, eh?"

I narrowed my eyes at her, reaching out a hand, but Mee-maw was faster, snatching one from the tray and shoving the whole thing into her mouth, chewing furiously.

I tried to grab one, as well, but Zoe pulled the tray away from me. "We should see how invisible it makes her before eating these ones, I have some other batches in the fridge in case this one isn't as strong."

"What are the other effects?" Mee-maw asked casually, as if it'd been merely an afterthought.

"Nothing too bad," Zoe said, shrugging, "but I want to see what you experience before telling you what I felt, to see if they line up."

I found myself pacing, looking periodically at Mee-maw to see if the potion had taken effect. It started after a few minutes with a gradual fading but, at about the ten-minute mark, I looked up at a gasp from Patrick, looking around for where she'd gone, to realize that she was invisible. Not just kind of transparent, but totally and truly invisible.

"Whoahhh," Mee-maw said, her voice sounding much softer than usual, "this feels strange. You guys look somehow fuzzy and out of focus, and it's almost like my clothes are heavier."

"What do you mean?" I asked. What a weird side effect for a potion to have. "You're kind of quiet, too."

"I noticed the clothes thing when I tried them, as well," Zoe said, nodding sagely. "The body seems to become weaker in proportion to how invisible the muffin makes you, so it's good to hear that you still have *some* strength. I thought about it for a long while but couldn't figure out how invisibility and all those weird side effects are related."

"I've read about this," Mee-maw said, almost inaudibly. "I think the potion weakens the body's connection to our plane of existence. That'd explain why I can still see my own body clearly while you guys seem a little blurry, as well."

"That makes a lot of sense," Zoe said, nodding.

I rolled my eyes, feeling a surge of annoyance as I walked back over to her, grabbing a muffin. "Let's all eat one so we can get moving once the effects set in. We can pack extras in case they wear off."

Zoe nodded, her tired eyes growing more serious as she reached in, biting into a muffin of her own. "You're right."

"Great job, by the way," I added, nodding appreciatively at her. She'd always been someone I could rely on and this was no exception. And she'd been clutch today when I needed her most.

Patrick walked up to the muffins, eyeing them with suspicion. "Are we sure it's safe? It doesn't sound like a good idea to weaken our connection to our realm or whatever you guys were saying." I shot him a sharp glance, however, and he picked one up, taking a big bite out of it, shaking his head while we ate. We both knew he was in no position to refuse and he'd never have let the rest of us go without him anyway.

My palate exploded with cinnamon-y flavor as I bit into the muffin.

"This tastes really good," Patrick said grudgingly, taking the words out of my mouth as he ate the last piece of his muffin.

Zoe nodded with a thin smile. "Of course th--" She turned her head, her eyes narrowing as another knock sounded at the door.

We'd put a big sign on the door saying that the bakery was closed, and all the windows were covered so you couldn't see inside, so why was someone knocking?

I popped the rest of the muffin into my mouth and walked over, pulling the curtains on one of the windows a few inches to the side to see who it was. I swallowed, pausing for a second in confusion before turning to Zoe. "Phil," I mouthed.

"Crap," Zoe said, rubbing her temples. "He's not even supposed to be back in town yet. If he finds me not here and not home, we're asking for trouble. Let him in for a sec. We have at least five minutes before the muffins start to work."

I walked over to the door, opening it slightly. "Hey, Phil, what's up?"

"Can I come in? I need to talk to my wife," he said, gesturing inside.

"Uh, sure," I said, my mind racing. If Mee-maw's test run was anything to go by, we only had a few minutes before the invisibility muffins kicked in, and Phil could *not* be here when they did.

"What's going on?" Phil said, scrunching his nose as he looked around at the bakery, which clearly hadn't been used for actual baking in some time. "I've been calling since last night."

"My phone broke," Zoe blurted. She still looked like she was about to collapse from exhaustion. "What are you doing home already?"

"Conference ended early. That's why I was calling last night. And the shop?" Phil asked, looking around. "Why'd you close it?"

"It's being fumigated," Zoe said, pointing to Patrick, "he's the exterminator."

I cringed at the lie. Patrick was sitting down, muffin wrapper in front of him, and was dressed in a t-shirt and jeans.

"Fumigated for what?" Phil said in his normal impassive tone, like he really couldn't care less about what was happening to the bakery but knew he had to ask anyway, though he did keep one suspicious eye on Patrick.

There was a short pause so I piped in to help. "Rats."

Zoe glared at me, shaking her head and forcing a laugh. "Hahaha, rats. Like anyone would come back to a bakery that was rumored to be teeming with rats. No...it's termites, actually, Cricket is just being silly."

I cringed at the reprimand but nodded.

"Oh," Phil said, his face lighting up as he looked at the muffin tray that was sitting on the counter, "any chance I could snag one of those muffins?"

"Uhh," Zoe said, a look of pure terror coming across her

face, "they're really not any good, I was just testing a new recipe."

Phil walked forward. "Let me try one, I'm sure they're great."

Zoe pulled the tray behind her defensively. "I need the rest of these for...a gift."

"A gift of bad muffins?" he said, beginning to look very suspicious, though he stopped moving to grab one. "You're acting very strangely. Speaking of that, what's up with the house? I stopped home before I came here and it looks like nobody has been there in days."

I could see the gears turning in Zoe's sleep-deprived brain for a long moment before she came up with something to say. "Phil, I didn't want to do this now, with everyone around, but I think we need to take a break. I've been staying with Mee-maw and Cricket. I just have a lot of things to think about."

Oof. It was imperative that we get him to leave, but this felt a bit rough, even to me, and I hated Phil. On the upside, however, maybe she'd actually go through with it once this whole Organization mess was all over.

"A break?" Phil said, with a frown. "Is that the real reason I haven't been able to get in touch with you?"

Zoe thought for a moment and her face went from blank to angry. "Yes, Phil, now get out. I need some time alone."

"Alone? You're alone all the time. We hardly even see each other," he said, looking more confused than anything else. "Was it the whole anniversary thing again? I told you, I'm really sorry. I'm not good with dates..."

I shrugged, remembering when I'd been in a high school play as I threw myself into it. "Leave her alone, Phil! Zoe said she doesn't want to see you right now, so get out of here!"

He blinked at me. "Okay, okay, I get it, but can we at least figure out some time to talk about everything?"

Sweat broke out on my upper lip as I began to feel my shirt weighing down on my shoulders. Was it just my imagination or...? I looked back to Phil and realized that we had very little time left. He was beginning to look fuzzy, almost blurry, to my eyes.

"No means no, Phil!" I shouted, stomping toward him and forcing Phil out the door.

"Wait, I--"

Patrick pushed him out, slamming the door in his face. "The lady said go," he ground out, locking it behind him.

I let out a relieved sigh, though I did feel a little guilty.

"Phew," Zoe said after a few seconds, "good job, guys. It felt crappy to do that to him but it was the only way. I'll have to make it up to him somehow once we're done with all this."

"Or, you could just, you know, leave it. Let him move on with his life," I added with a hopeful smile.

She rolled her eyes and then stilled at the tapping at the covered window and I turned, confused. "You're still here?" Zoe called, walking over to the window and peering out.

"Sorry," Phil said, "I just had to ask...Are you still going to pick up my dry cleaning later?"

"This stuff is incredible," I said, whispering as we slipped right past a pedestrian. We could all see each other perfectly but everyone else looked like you were seeing them through a foggy window. The potion's noise cancelling effects were also quite useful and nobody had noticed us, even when we'd walked right in front of them.

"Thanks," Zoe said, grinning.

"It'll definitely come in handy," Patrick said grudgingly,

"assuming nobody ends up getting stuck in a different plane of existence or anything."

Mee-maw glanced down at her compass, a deadly serious look on her face. "I really hope the item is somewhere in Rocky Knoll."

"I have a feeling it will be," I said. "Connie wouldn't send it too far away and the compass is starting to seem like it's moving a lot, even if we go just a little bit out of the way, so it seems like we're getting close."

"I can't wait to see what it is," Mee-maw said, rubbing her hands together. "Maybe it'll be a knife or a sword or something cool like that."

I laughed. "You have anything in the world to draw from and you'd want a magic knife?"

"It'd be sweet," she said, turning her nose up at me and pointing for us to take a right. "Over this way."

We turned the corner and a huge building popped into view, filling my field of vision. I read the name at the top and everything snapped into place.

The Rocky Knoll Museum of Local History

"Looks like we found your item," I said, smiling. We'd be a hell of a lot closer to defeating the Organization and protecting my family if we could just use our invisibility to grab Mee-maw's item and move on with our plan.

"Looks like it," Mee-maw said, speeding up to march as she made a beeline toward the entrance.

I sped up behind her, quickly closing the distance to the stairs with Zoe and Patrick in tow.

"But how do we get inside?" Patrick asked with a look of pain on his face. I'd have to change the bandage again when we got back, there was no doubt that this much movement was bad for his wound.

"I guess we have to try to break in--" I cut off, my heart

sinking as I saw the huge sign that sat next to the two doors. *Closed to Public Access Until Further Notice.* As we got closer, I saw the smaller text below it: *Contact the office of Ethan Morrisey for information.*
Ethan.
"I have an idea!"

CHAPTER 17

WE HAD SCOOTED off into a nearby copse of trees to make sure we were out of sight, as our potion had begun to wear off slightly, but Mee-maw hadn't taken her eyes off the museum in the distance, like a kid waiting for the toy store to open. Patrick stood a few yards away, absently rubbing his chest and looking generally annoyed. I had a feeling his irritation was more due to my plan than it was about his wound. It wasn't bleeding, as far as I could see, but his discomfort was obvious, and I felt a pang of sympathy for him. When we got back to the bakery, I'd talk to Zoe about trying to come up with a healing potion for him. He might not be willing to take it, but maybe if I played on his protective nature and told him we needed him at his strongest, I'd have a shot. As far as his feelings on the plan?

Tough tacos.

He was going to have to deal. Ethan was the path of least resistance and, as much as I hated using him, the close call at Greg's house had lit a fire within me. We needed to get this coven bonded tight and strong so we could take down the Organization for good.

I pulled out my burner phone and dialed Ethan's number. It felt like it weighed about ten pounds in my hand, no doubt due to the invisibility potion that was only just starting to wear off. Putting it up to my ear was like lifting a dumbbell, and took both hands.

The phone began to ring in my ear and I mentally ran through what I would say when Ethan picked up.

"How do you know he'll even be available?" Zoe protested, her arm going fuzzy and then clear again and out of view. "Plus, you kinda ghosted him after he caught you snooping at his house."

I waved her away as the phone rang again—four times, five— and I was starting to wonder if Zoe was right, when a familiar voice sounded on the other end.

"Ethan Morrisey."

"Hi, Ethan!" I said, a rush of relief coursing through me. *One obstacle down.* "It's Cricket."

"Sorry, who?" he asked, a little louder. "Can you speak up. I'm having a hard time hearing you."

Drat.

I should've waited until the potion had worn off completely before making the call.

Glancing at the others, I tried again, a little louder. "Ethan! It's Cricket!"

"Cricket? Is that you?" He sounded confused. "I think our connection is bad. I can barely hear you."

"Sorry, is this better?" It felt like I was basically shouting, which made the call all the more awkward with the others all listening in, but I could only assume if someone did happen to be in the vicinity, I'd seem quiet to them, as well.

"Yeah," he replied. "Yeah, that's better."

There was a long pause as I shoved aside a surge of both

guilt and anxiety. "So, ah..." I cleared my throat. "Sorry I haven't called. It's been a few days!"

"Yeah, it has." He sounded guarded now. "I was starting to think I'd done something to offend you on our date."

"No, no, not at all," I replied quickly. I glanced over at Patrick, who was watching me with unabashed interest. "I promise it wasn't that. Things have been kind of crazy lately."

"Well, is everything okay?" he asked, his tone changing on a dime to one of concern.

God, I hated this. Once the Organization was ground into dust, I was swearing off lying for good.

"I tried calling you a couple times the past few days, and it went straight to voice mail. Then, I stopped by your Mee-maw's just to check in on her and say hi. There were cars in the driveway, but no one came to the door. I was really starting to wonder what was going on when I went to the bakery to get lunch and found it closed. It didn't sound like there was any renovation happening, as far as I could hear. No trucks out front, no one working inside."

"Fumigation!" I exclaimed, a little too quickly, sparing a pointed glance at Zoe. "*Termites*. We had to shut the whole thing down before it got out of hand, and I've been helping her. You won't believe this, but I actually sent my phone through the wash, so I had to get a cheap pay per call one until I can get around to replacing mine." I raked a hand through my hair. "Listen, Ethan, I'm really sorry. I didn't mean to leave you high and dry like that. Everything has gotten out of control." *You have no idea,* I added mentally, closing my eyes for a moment.

"It's all right," he said, sounding genuinely relieved, which just made my guilt worse. "I was worried something had happened to you. Or Mee-maw. How is she, by the way?"

"She's still kicking," I replied, glancing at my grandmother, whose eyes were still glued to the museum entrance. "Probably a little *too* well, all things considered."

Ethan chuckled. "Well, I guess I shouldn't be surprised by that. Tell her I said hello, would you?"

"Of course. So Ethan--"

"Look," he said, "I've got some things to catch up on here but I can be done in an hour and I'd really like to see you. How about lunch and a movie? There's this falafel place down on Main Street that just opened, and I've heard is excellent. It could be fun."

"That does sound fun," I replied with a forced chuckle. Out of the corner of my eye, I caught Patrick stiffening almost imperceptibly. "But I'm kind of in the thick of it right now at the bakery. Zoe and I are...um, handling the fumigating ourselves. And then there's the ones that don't die. Those little buggers are fast so it's a lot of...wrangling. And stuff, too." Weird how, despite the muffled voices, I could still hear Mee-maw's and Zoe's collective groan. "Anyway, until that's done in a few days, I'm pretty much at her beck and call. Can I take a rain check for next week?"

"Okay," Ethan replied. He sounded disappointed, but he was hiding it well. "But be careful. Those fumes aren't good to be breathing in..."

"We have masks and all, so it's fine." I swallowed hard and pushed on. "I was actually calling for another reason," I continued, feeling crappier by the second.

"Shoot," he replied gamely.

I pinched the bridge of my nose. "Is your family still the primary benefactor of the Rocky Knoll Historical Society?"

"I mean...yeah," he responded, sounding surprised. "Technically, at least. My parents let the whole project slide for years. I think they just liked having their names attached to it, but they never seemed to care much about the actual artifacts. I just took over for them recently. I'm in the midst of renovating. Why do you ask?"

"I have this friend," I explained, the wheels in my head whirring. "She's actually our local librarian, and she's big on historical programs. She was hoping to collaborate with the museum for an exhibition and talk she's doing at the library." I crossed my fingers, praying he'd buy the hastily-crafted excuse.

"Really?"

I could practically hear the excitement in his voice.

Got him.

"That's fantastic!" Reeling himself back a little, he added, sounding sheepish, "I mean, that's great to hear. I'm a big history buff—I'm all about that stuff. It seems like no one's really cared much about the museum, so this could be a great way to get some buzz before the reopening in the Spring, too." There was a pause. "What's the lecture topic?"

Crap.

"Uh...artifacts. Town artifacts and their origin...some genealogy thrown in there."

"Genealogy?"

I needed to wrap this up ASAP. I was drowning in my own deception.

"I mean, in the context of Rocky Knoll—important people in the town's history, family trees, that sort of thing. Your family's been around here for ages, and I'm sure the museum is chock full of amazing artifacts, so it seemed kind of a match made in heaven."

"It does." He sounded intrigued. "We've got loads of stuff. When is the exhibition scheduled for? I can meet up with her next week sometime--"

"Day after tomorrow, actually. The exhibition is the day after tomorrow. Guh, I'm so sorry about the short notice," I replied, my cheeks flaming as I pressed on. "I told her not to get her hopes up, but I'd ask and cross my fingers. She has this whole show she puts on for the little kids that come, to try to get them interested in history. She uses puppets and stuff." I could feel the weight of Patrick's stare like a brick on my chest and wished I could find a hole to dive into. "She was just hoping to have a few cool-looking items for them to see, but you know what? I didn't give you enough notice. And, hey, those kids might as well get used to being disappointed, right? That will prepare them for the real world."

"No, no, not at all," Ethan said in a rush. "I can work something out. The stuff just sits there. It's meant to be for the community to enjoy and learn from. When were you thinking?"

"I was hoping it would be possible to take a spin through today, just to get a sense of what she's working with. And to make sure it all jives with you, obviously."

"I can do that," Ethan answered. "As I mentioned, I've got a meeting to finish up here, but I could swing by in about an hour if she's available."

She sure better be.

"Perfect. I'll call her and let her know. Her name is Trudy."

"Sounds good." There was a long pause. "And, Cricket? Make sure you put our rain check date on your calendar. I can't stop thinking about you since our kiss the other night."

I bit my lip, willing my face not to spontaneously combust as I aggressively avoided Patrick's gaze. "Yes. I'll surely do that. Thank you so much, Ethan. I really appreciate it."

"No problem. I'll talk to you soon."

I hung up before turning to look at the others, who were waiting for an update. "Ethan's going to come open the place up," I told them, already dialing the librarian's number on the burner phone. "We're going to need to get Trudy over here, too."

"Yes, well, we wouldn't want to disappoint the kids," Zoe deadpanned.

I ignored her until Trudy picked up on the second ring.

"Cricket," she said. "What's going on?"

"We think we've found my grandma's magical item," I replied.

"That's fantastic! Where is it?"

"That's the thing," I explained. "It's in the history museum, but the place is closed for construction. I told a friend of mine you were interested in putting an exhibit together, and he's willing to come show you around. We're going to follow you in and, when Mee-maw locates the item, we're going to nab it. Zoe found a way to make us invisible."

"Awesome," she breathed. It was like I had given her the best news in the world. "This I have to see."

"You will," I assured her. "I mean, not *see*, exactly, but..." I shook my head. "Ethan should be here in about an hour."

"Where are you guys now?"

"We're here already," I replied, rattling off the address.

"Got it, I know where it is," Trudy replied, a woman on a mission. "Be there shortly."

We waited outside the museum, Patrick standing a short distance away while Mee-maw and Zoe paced. Twenty minutes before their scheduled arrival, we each popped another muffin. I found myself glancing down over and over, not just to check my phone for the time, but also to make sure we were fully invisible again; the last thing we needed right now was for Trudy—or, god forbid, Ethan—to stumble across us when we were starting to flicker back into view.

After checking the burner for what felt like the millionth time, I looked up to see Ethan getting out of his car and strolling up to the front doors. My hand flew out, taking Mee-maw by the arm and guiding her out of the way moments before he came to a stop right where she had been standing. He shuffled his feet, checking his watch and putting his hands in his pockets, completely unaware of the fact that there were four others within feet of him. It was weird, but at least it didn't last long; a few minutes later, Trudy's minivan rolled to a stop in the parking lot, and we watched her clamber out.

For a second, I thought her car had been stolen by a woman around her height and size. Gone were the tight, mousy bun and ill-fitting rooster clothing; her hair tumbled in soft waves around her shoulders, her face was tastefully done in neutral makeup, complete with glossy lips, her dress was a curve-hugging knockout in black, complete with jewelry and a handbag. She was dressed to the nines, as if she had been waiting for this moment her entire life—and for all I knew, she had been.

She's pretty, I realized with a start. Could this really have been the same uptight woman with pinched gaze and the demeanor of a middle school teacher who we had first encountered at the library?

Mee-maw and I exchanged a look, and I could read the expression on her face loud and clear.

She cleans up nicely.

Trudy's appearance wasn't lost on Ethan, either; he actually did a mini-double-take as she approached. "You must be Trudy," he said with a warm smile as he held out his hand.

Trudy gave him a firm handshake. "And you must be Ethan. I really appreciate you doing this for me, especially on a workday. I was hoping you wouldn't have to go too far out of your way." She was really turning on the charm.

"Don't worry about it," Ethan assured her. "I'm not far from downtown, actually. It's fantastic to meet someone else who's interested in this town's history."

"Oh, I absolutely am," Trudy replied, smiling. "I think this could end up being a really fun project."

There was a pause, and then Ethan cleared his throat.

"Well, shall we, then? I've never really given a *tour* of the place, per se, but..."

"That's all right," she told him. "In fact, I think it would be better if we just sort of poked around the whole place. I'm not really sure what I'm going for yet, so maybe you could give me some ideas."

"It would be my pleasure."

Ethan fumbled with a set of keys for a moment before opening the front door and leading Trudy in. She followed slowly, lingering off to the side long enough for us to come through before she stepped in. She was squinting every once in a while, clearly trying to catch sight of us, but other than that, she kept her cool as we padded behind them.

Mee-maw held her compass out in front of her, eyes glued to it.

"It starts with the ancient history of the area and then works forward into modern times," Ethan was saying as he and Trudy began to navigate the winding hallways as we trailed a few yards behind them. Shelves of artifacts and knick-knacks covered the walls, along with old maps and a couple of interactive exhibits; any of them could have been Mee-maw's item. It was like looking for a needle in a haystack. Luckily, if she was anything like Zoe and I, she'd know it when she saw it.

"Did you know that Rocky Knoll started out with a population of just around twenty?"

"I did!" Trudy replied, her face lighting up. "All fishermen and tradespeople."

I crept up behind Mee-maw, peering over her shoulder. The compass needle was pointed stiffly towards the end of the hallway. Carefully, we moved forward, struggling to give Ethan and Trudy a wide berth.

"So," Ethan was saying, pausing at a diorama, "what do you think?"

"Of their costumes? They seem authentic."

He paused for dramatic affect and then grinned. "They are."

She gaped at him. "You're kidding!"

Ethan laughed, shaking his head. "Nope. These were actually bequeathed by my grandfather. Been in the family since the 1700s."

Trudy was doing a bang-up job of keeping him engaged. That was good, because we needed time. So far, the only thing we had to go on was the insistence of Mee-maw's compass.

"Anything?" I whispered, putting a hand on her arm.

She shook her head. "We're just going to have to follow the darned thing. I don't even know how I'll recognize it when I see it."

"Try sensing for it," Zoe suggested. "Feel for it."

"What am I supposed to be 'feeling for', exactly?"

Zoe looked to me for backup. "Something you sense a connection with," I said. "Something that draws you in, you know?"

"Like a really good sale on olive loaf?" Mee-maw asked.

"Sure, if that's what floats your boat," I said with a shrug, starting to wonder if I'd made a misstep here. Maybe she was too far past menopause to find her item like Zoe and I had.

The thought made me unbearably sad for a moment. Losing to the Organization and dying would suck most. But Mee-maw never getting a taste of her magic when she was made to be a witch would be almost as tragic.

"Come on, Mee-maw, focus," I urged, blinking my suddenly stinging eyes.

She sniffed, frowning, but closed her eyes, coming to a stop with the compass in her hands. There was a long moment of silence, and her brow furrowed in concentration, but moments later, she sighed, looked up, and shook her head.

"I'm sorry, I got nothing," she muttered.

I pursed my lips as we continued to follow Ethan and Trudy deeper into the bowels of the museum, my confidence dropping with every step we took.

Maybe this wasn't going to be as easy as we had thought...

CHAPTER 18

"Dang it!" Mee-maw hissed, coming to a stop so suddenly that I almost ran right into her, causing Zoe to nearly trip over me in the process.

"What is it?" I hissed, creeping up alongside Mee-maw.

"Nothing," Mee-maw replied. "I just remembered, I think I might have left the coffee pot on back at the bakery."

Zoe let out a frustrated groan. "How is that relevant right now, Mee-maw?"

"Well, forgive me for being conscientious! Geez."

"Both of you shush," I hissed. "They're going to hear us."

"Oh, relax." She waved me off. "We're muffled. Plus, those two wouldn't hear a plane crashing into Town Square with the way they're carrying on."

As if on cue, a peal of laughter came from the next room over, where we could see Ethan showing Trudy a map from Colonial-era Rocky Knoll.

"If you think that's cool," he said, grinning at her and raising a brow, "do you want to see the section on the Revolutionary War?"

"I thought you would never ask," Trudy replied, shouldering

her bag, and the two of them started heading for the next room on the right.

"Come on," I said, tugging at Mee-maw's wrist.

"Like hell," she exclaimed, showing me the compass. "This thing's telling me to head that way."

She was right. The needle was rigid and unmoving, pointing directly in the opposite direction they were going. Patrick moved to the door and tried it, but it was no use; most of the rooms were still locked up, and the invisibility potion had already taken a toll on our physical strength. There was no way of getting in if we weren't following Ethan and Trudy.

I exchanged a panicked look with Zoe before the four of us turned and raced into the other room, just as Ethan was unlocking the door. Trudy was peering around, squinting every so often, no doubt wondering where we were.

"Trudy," I called, "you guys are going the wrong way!" The librarian stopped in her tracks, raising an eyebrow and looking around suspiciously. "Trudy," I tried again, and her brow furrowed as if a mosquito had just buzzed past her ear. "She can't hear me," I realized despairingly. Yelling at her would risk catching Ethan's attention, and he was already heading through the door; in moments, we would be locked out.

Not thinking, I rushed forward, giving her a swift nudge with my foot. Trudy leapt into the air like she'd gotten an electric shock, which would have been almost comical if she hadn't shrieked at the same time.

Ethan whirled around. "Are you okay?"

"I..." She stammered for a moment, staring at me—or rather, at what, no doubt, looked to her like an empty space, one that had just kicked her out of nowhere. "Cricket?" she whispered, her eyes wide with shock. If I didn't know any better, I might have even thought that she could see me. At a loss, I could only repeat the nudge I had given her by way of confirmation.

"Did you just say Cricket?" Ethan asked, his head cocked. By now, he had come back over and put a concerned hand on Trudy's shoulder.

"No? Yes." Trudy stared at him blankly for a moment, and my heart sank. She shook her head as if a nest of wasps had taken up residence in her hair. "I thought it was a cricket but it's a mouse!"

"Mice?" Ethan's eyebrows shot up. "Where?"

Trudy nodded. "Two of them! They went, uh…" She turned her attention back to me, and I gave her sleeve a desperate tug in the right direction. "That way!" Jabbing a finger in the direction the compass was pointing, she rushed on. "I've heard they sometimes make burrows in the foundations of these buildings. It happened back at the library once, actually."

I had to give her props for her improvisation, in spite of her earlier stumbles; Ethan's face was a picture of worry.

"That's not good," he said, running a hand through his hair. "I'm so sorry to do this, I know you wanted to see the Revolutionary War room next, but I need to see if they've done any major damage. We have a lot of fragile old books and documents."

"I don't mind at all," Trudy replied, putting up a hand. "We should make sure that's taken care of before they get to anything important."

I could feel my heartbeat slowly returning to normal as the duo turned around and started in the opposite direction. Meemaw and Zoe scampered out of the line of fire, narrowly avoiding getting bumped into as they made their way back into the hallway, Ethan pausing at the door on the left to dig out his keys.

"I don't see any holes or droppings…" he murmured.

"They can fit under doors with even the smallest cracks.

You'd be surprised," Trudy replied hastily. "The ones at the library ate into the flooring and everything."

"Great," he muttered, pinching the bridge of his nose. "More renovations. Well, better now than later, I guess. Here..." He unlocked the door and pushed it open just as Trudy sidled up to him.

"What room is this?" she asked as she followed him through, taking her sweet time to allow the rest of us time to enter.

"This is the storage area," Ethan replied, flipping on a light switch. We found ourselves in a windowless room lit by fluorescent bulbs. Stainless steel shelves and work tables lined the walls, all scattered with plastic-covered documents and artifacts. It was eerie seeing it deserted like this. "This is where we keep all the items that haven't been properly authenticated or documented," he explained, stooping a little to check under one of the tables. "It's also where they do all the cleaning and restoration, although we've had to put it on hold while the renovation is happening."

"Wow," Trudy breathed, and one look at her expression was enough to tell me that she wasn't faking her wonder.

We couldn't have picked a better person for this job, I thought, unable to keep from smiling a little.

Seemingly coming back to herself, she cleared her throat and stole a glance over her shoulder, as if expecting us to suddenly be visible. "Maybe we should start in the far corner," she suggested. "Lots of hiding places in a room like this."

"Good idea," Ethan said. "You're not afraid of mice, are you?"

"Not...usually. I was just startled," the librarian replied, swallowing. "Besides," she pressed on, "I've got you, right?"

"I'll do my best to protect you," Ethan agreed, chuckling, and the two of them began their vermin search at the back of the room.

I hung back, coming to stand beside the others, who were all staring at the librarian with newfound admiration.

"Jeez," Mee-maw muttered. "I didn't think we'd get here this quickly. She really knows how to turn on the charm—and she didn't even have to flash her cans or anything!"

Patrick snorted, and then, seeing the look I gave him, tried to disguise it with a cough.

"They're on the move, let's go," Mee-maw said, squaring her shoulders. Holding the compass out like a dowsing rod, she began to move through the confined space, never taking her eyes off the quivering needle.

"Are you feeling anything?" Zoe asked in a low voice.

"My ankles are acting up something fierce," Mee-maw replied, "but otherwise...Wait a minute." She stopped, narrowing her eyes, and sniffed—actually *sniffed*—the air like some kind of bloodhound. "I think I have something," she muttered.

"What is it?" I asked, eyes wide.

There was a long pause as Mee-maw continued to sniff the air. "Never mind," she said at last. "Just dust bunnies and old books."

I let out a long sigh. "You have to concentrate." I was practically pleading with her now; Zoe was just learning and the potions had been dicey, at best. And even with Trudy working her charms, Ethan couldn't be stalled forever.

"Try to reach out with your mind," I suggested, staring down at an old painting on one of the work tables. "You have to be open to it, Mee-maw!"

"I *am* being open to it," she snapped. "You can't blame me for--" but then she stopped and frowned, looking from the compass to one of the shelves on the wall a few yards away, where a three-foot by three-foot velvet box lay, collecting dust. "It's there," she whispered.

"Are you sure?" asked Zoe, her tone tense. "What does the compass say?"

"It went crazy," Mee-maw replied. "The needle started bouncing around like it was possessed, and then it just locked onto that over there." She pointed to a shelf marked 1600-1700.

"Well, what are we waiting for?" asked Patrick. "Let's grab the box while their backs are turned."

I moved toward it but then stopped short in horror as I caught something flickering in the corner of my eye.

Mee-maw.

The noncorporeal air about her was lessening, and I could see with rising panic that her body was beginning to take form again, flickering from translucent to solid, like a developing polaroid.

This was not good.

"Abort, abort!" I hissed.

"What?" she demanded, turning around. "I have to—oh my lord, Cricket, you're turning solid!" She glanced down at herself. "And so am I!"

Trudy whirled around at that, her face pale as her gaze flicked around our general area; clearly our voices were starting to return to this plane, as well. Her gaze locked with mine, and I gave a quick shake of my head, hoping she saw it before I disappeared again.

"Ethan! I think I saw one run behind that trashcan," she shrieked.

Trudy the librarian was clutch.

"Go, go, go," I hissed at the others as Trudy urged Ethan onto all fours in search of a non-existent mouse and we made a dash for the door.

"What about the box?" Zoe asked, in hot pursuit.

"No time," I replied in an agitated whisper. "We'll text Trudy to nab it."

I turned to see how far behind Mee-maw was, and skidded to a stop, my heart skipping a beat when I realized she wasn't behind me at all. She'd made her way toward the shelf, her eyes locked on the box like she was in a trance.

"I don't see anything," Ethan said, standing up and turning around, hands on his hips, his gaze moving steadily in our direction.

But a split second later, Trudy grabbed his arm, dragging him back around to face her.

"Sorry," she said with a shrill chuckle. "You've got a little smudge of something on your jaw. Your, ah...very...handsome... jaw." She licked her finger and began rubbing at the imaginary spot, jerking her head sharply towards the door as she did.

Zoe lunged toward Mee-maw, snatching her wrist and pulling her out the door.

"You know," Trudy was saying, "maybe it would be better to just call an exterminator. I think the little buggers are going to hide until the lights go out again anyway."

"Maybe you're right," Ethan acknowledged. "I'm sorry you had to deal with this. We're not exactly making the best first impression, here."

Their voices faded as we made a mad dash for the main entrance, our physical forms returning more every second. By the time we reached the doors, getting them open was no problem. Ten seconds later, we were bolting back down the walkway. Zoe had her arm linked with Mee-maw, and I realized with surprise that I had taken hold of Patrick's hand without even being aware of it. We shared a glance and he gave my hand a reassuring squeeze as we rounded a corner into the parking lot. The copse of trees where we'd been hiding earlier wasn't far, and by the time we were under the shelter of their branches, we were more or less visible again.

"Crap," I muttered, leaning forward and putting my hands

on my knees. I was breathing hard, and my nerves were shot. One glance up at Zoe and Patrick told me the same. "We were so frigging close."

"Why didn't you just let me grab it?" Mee-maw demanded.

"It's a big box and we have no clue what's inside or if we could have lifted it in our condition. If we dropped it, we'd have been busted."

Mee-maw nodded miserably, realizing the truth of my words.

"So now what?" Zoe asked, putting her hands on her hips.

"More muffins?" Patrick suggested with a hint of reluctance.

"Too late for that," Zoe replied, pointing, and I turned around to see Trudy and Ethan emerging from the museum, chatting amiably.

I groaned. It had been *right there*. A few more seconds and it would've been ours.

I fired off a quick message to Trudy.

We're in the trees on the west side of the parking lot. Come meet us when Ethan is gone.

We waited in defeated silence until the librarian arrived a few minutes later. "Sorry, he wanted to get in touch with the exterminator ASAP, and I wasn't sure whether you already got the item or not, so I didn't want to keep stalling like an idiot."

We were all silent as she eyed us questioningly. "Well?"

Patrick shook his head with a frown. "Nope. It was in a velvet box on a shelf with artifacts from the 17th century, but we didn't have time to nab it."

Trudy's face fell. "Really? I wasn't sure...I saw a flicker of Cricket and Mee-maw, but I didn't know what to do."

"It's fine," Zoe assured her. "You did great. And hey, at least we know it's here. We can break in later tonight or something..."

I sighed and shook my head.

"Not being able to use our full strength is a major roadblock on that front. One we don't have time for right now." I wheeled around and kicked a nearby stone with a growl. "Why does everything have to be so hard?"

"I don't know, but I'm sure glad I implemented Plan B," Trudy said, a hopeful smile spreading across her face.

We'd barely taken the time to concoct a Plan A.

"What's Plan B?"

"We actually have an exhibition. I've already set it up with Ethan. He asked me to send him a list of everything I want on loan from the museum. And what I want on display is everything he's got from the 17th century, when Rocky Knoll was first established."

Clutch.

CHAPTER 19

WAITING for the exhibition had been interminable, but at least we knew we were heading in the right direction. The compass had started to move as soon as Ethan brought his stuff to the library, which meant this part of our nightmare was almost over.

In theory, anyway—given my luck, I didn't want to get my hopes up too high, especially when every time we hit a break, something always seemed to fall apart at the last second.

It had been two days since our failed attempt at locating Mee-maw's item. Two days, which had felt like an eternity as we were sidelined while Trudy scrambled to help Ethan get ready for the exhibition.

The librarian had been a pleasant surprise amidst everything else, and the fact that she was solely responsible for giving us a second shot at our search wasn't lost on me. She'd been an integral part of the team, and it made me feel a little more settled at having heeded Maude's words about opening our circle of trust and including her. I made a mental note to do something to thank her for all her help when all this was over—if it was ever over.

Despite the delay, the four of us were finally sitting in the two rows of back seats in an Uber that we had called to pick us up from the alleyway behind the bakery to take us to the exhibition that afternoon; it wouldn't pay to get sloppy, even with a police officer keeping an eye on the place at night.

"Everybody feeling all right? No bad joo-joo or anything?" Patrick asked, turning around in his middle row seat to look back at me, casting a wary glance at the Uber driver who was in the midst of a heated conversation in Russian on his headset.

He certainly wasn't paying us any mind, which was good. I let out a long sigh, shaking my head. "My gut is as silent as Maude is on the topic. I think we're on the right path, or she would've warned me, but who can say for sure?"

"It's gonna be fine. I'm gonna get my item, and then we're getting the hell out of Dodge," Mee-maw added, crossing her arms. "I've heard Cabo is nice this time of year."

"For the last time, Mee-maw, we're not going to Cabo," Zoe replied, sounding exasperated.

"Why not? I've never been."

"Wouldn't it be better to just pick a direction and go?" I suggested. "The less predictable we can be, the easier it will be to shake the Organization. I hope."

Truth be told, the idea of just up and leaving wasn't my favorite, but I liked the idea of sticking around like sitting ducks before we had all truly gotten a handle on our powers even less. So we had spent the last day making plans to leave town for a while. As soon as we had Mee-maw's item, we would be in the wind, on a long cross-country road trip, away from the prying eyes of the Organization, to give us some time to get Mee-maw up to speed. It wasn't exactly an easy prospect, and Zoe was already planning on tapping into the cash she kept at the bakery. Patrick had also offered up a good chunk of cash—enough to hold us over for a while if we stretched it—which meant we would have ample time to find someplace remote where we could all practice our magic until the coven was at its full power.

I had to remind myself that this wasn't me running away—it was running, sure, but we were going to come back, stronger than ever.

Strong enough to take down the Organization and make sure that what almost happened to me never happened to anyone again.

"Cricket's right," Patrick agreed. "We're going to have to find somewhere off the grid."

Zoe held up a hand as she watched the passing town outside the window. "One thing at a time."

For her part, my cousin had been feverishly working on new potions—mostly in the form of baked goods—that might be useful to us. It was an exhaustive amount of trial and error, but considering how well her invisibility spell had worked, it looked like she was really starting to get the hang of it. Trudy had been in touch with us, mostly via the burner phones, as she worked on organizing the event with Ethan, doing a bang-up job, all things considered.

She had initially tried to convince him to bring the display items to the library the day before, so we could get a private viewing and locate the item, easy peasy, but he had insisted on cleaning and prepping everything beforehand to make sure they would get a good showing and wasn't going to bring the items until the day of.

The tentative plan was for him and Trudy to set them up together today before the exhibit opened. It wasn't perfect, but at the end of the day, Trudy had already gone above and beyond and we couldn't complain.

We lapsed into silence once more as the car navigated the winding streets of downtown Rocky Knoll. The autumn weather was glorious—sunny and crisp—and a lot of people seemed to be out and about. Briefly, I felt a smidge of nostalgia—actual, honest-to-goodness nostalgia—for the days when my free time wasn't dictated by supernatural powers and shadowy organizations. When my idea of an eventful afternoon included a stroll by the pier or a happy hour gossip session with Zoe and a big, fat glass of cabernet. It was strange how quickly everything had seemed to blow up in my face, but that was partly why we were doing this. So that we could regain some semblance of a normal life instead of one spent constantly looking over our shoulders.

Well, that, and to save future witches from having their birthright stripped from them and hung by their necks until they were dead.

The feeling of a gentle touch on my hand was enough to draw me from my depressing but motivating reminder, and I looked up to see Patrick watching me.

"Sure you're okay?" he asked, his eyes meeting mine.

Since the night he'd comforted me after my nightmare and told me about his mother, we'd been dancing around one another. During the day, it had been a dance...moving close enough to touch, exchanging gazes packed with unsaid words, before one of us invariably pulled away. At night, we started out the same way, futon mats a yard apart by tacit agreement, but somehow we always wound up drifting closer together in the middle of the night, awakening wrapped in each other's arms.

I managed a tight smile, aware of Mee-maw and Zoe watching me. "Just ready to have this over with," I replied as we pulled to a stop in front of the library.

Almost as soon as I opened the door, I realized we'd vastly underestimated the number of people who would attend the event. We had arrived fifteen minutes early, and the library was already bustling with activity. Familiar and unfamiliar faces alike were flocking into the building, the sounds of music and easy chatter drifting over to us.

The crowd could be a good thing, on one hand—safety in numbers if the Organization saw the signs outside the library and sent someone to scout the place out. Or a bad thing, because we had more faces to scan as we searched, making them harder to spot if they did try to make a move.

"I'll be darned," Mee-maw said, shaking her head in disbelief as the Uber pulled away. "Who would've thought an exhibit about dead people and their antiques would draw such a crowd?"

"Beats me," I replied with a shrug. "And the whole thing was on such short notice..."

"Food," Zoe replied without missing a beat, nodding to a sign on the curb advertising apple cider donuts and coffee for the taking. "Event planning rule number one: give out treats and free coffee, and the blue hairs will come out in droves."

It was like she had said the magic word as, moments later, a flock of elderly ladies set their sights on Mee-maw, flocking over to us as we approached the library entrance.

I recognized a couple of them from Mee-maw's twice-a-week Bunko game, and a familiar competitive gleam appeared in my grandmother's eye as she stopped to say hello.

"There she is, in the flesh!" exclaimed one of them, sidling up next to her. "Priscilla and I were just wondering if you'd show up. See, I told you she wasn't dead," she added, elbowing the other woman triumphantly.

Mee-maw chuckled. "Nope. Still alive and kicking. I've been busy lately."

"Things are so much less interesting when you're not around! I heard you were having some problems with your ticker."

"Ladies, ladies," Mee-maw said, putting her hands up. "My

ticker is fine, Ann, thank you for asking," she added, turning a menacing look on the second woman. "Don't think you'll get rid of me that easily."

"Of course not!" cried the second woman. "You're the only one who can keep me on my toes."

Mee-maw laughed along with her through a thin smile. "I'll see you ladies inside, okay?"

She saw her Bunko group off, crossing her arms. "That was awfully...civil of you," Zoe observed. "Weren't you telling me you didn't want to play anymore on account of those two cheating?"

"Oh, sure," Mee-maw replied, "but that was before. I'm a witch now and, after today, I'm never going to lose at Bunko again."

I wanted to warn her that I wasn't sure it worked that way, but she looked so pleased, I didn't have the heart. Instead, I exchanged an eyeroll with Zoe as the four of us arrived at the makeshift admissions table, paid the entrance fee, and wandered inside.

It felt a little odd being back at the library during business hours, and even more so seeing it packed with townspeople. *Zoe wasn't kidding about the lure of a good donut*, I thought as a duo of housewives brushed past us, making a beeline for a display case housing a couple of antique books.

We were here on a mission, but I couldn't help but admire how much effort Trudy had put into making it legit. Tables and shelves ran up and down the corridors alongside detailed explanations and histories, mannequins in full seventeenth century regalia, and video projectors, all of which had been brought over from the museum. Classical music played over the speakers, and as we navigated the hallways, we passed by bins of specially-printed pamphlets and clusters of inquisitive townspeople. It was amazing to me how Trudy had accomplished all this in such a short amount of time—it really felt like a museum-level exhibition.

We had made it almost as far as the children's wing before we found the woman herself, dressed in a 1600s outfit that was a far cry from her usual ensemble. Her face lit up as soon as she saw us, and I watched as she disengaged from the cluster of children she'd been talking to before wandering over to us.

"There you are," she said, smiling. "I'm glad you're here!"

"So are we," Patrick replied, scanning the space around us. "This place looks awesome, Trudy. Seriously."

I nodded. "You did a fantastic job."

"Thanks," the librarian replied. "Ethan's really happy, too." It might have been the light, but I could have sworn I saw the faintest of blushes creep into her cheeks. "I felt a little bad, though," Trudy hurried on. "I don't know why, but it seems he was expecting a puppet show?"

Mee-maw raised her eyebrows at me but I just shrugged.

"That's weird...but, yeah. Truly awesome work."

At that moment, I caught a glimpse of Ethan making his way over to us, a wide smile on his face.

"People seem to really be enjoying it," I said, clearing my throat.

"They are," Ethan confirmed, coming to a stop next to Trudy. "I can hardly believe it. I've never seen people so psyched about the town history. It's going to give the reopening a huge boost, I think." There was a proud look in his eyes, which had come to rest on me. "You know, Cricket, if you want, I could show you around. We brought a ton of stuff in—there's even a record dating back to 1703."

"Well, that sounds..." I glanced from Patrick, who was watching the exchange with raised eyebrows, to Trudy, whose eyes were moving pointedly back and forth between our group and a cluster of display cases in the back corner. "That sounds great, Ethan," I stumbled on, "but I actually promised Zoe I'd stop for a donut first."

"Right," Zoe agreed. "I want to know if they used real apple cider in the dough. You can always tell."

His face fell a little. "No problem. Later, maybe."

"What about those old shipping manifests you mentioned yesterday?" Trudy put in. "I still haven't gotten a chance to look at them."

That seemed to do the trick, and Ethan smiled as he turned to her. "I almost forgot. I think they're back in the reference section, if I'm not mistaken."

We watched as he and Trudy wandered off, the librarian casting one last, long glance to the displays in the corner.

"That must be where the stuff from the velvet box is," Zoe said in a low voice as she glanced around us surreptitiously.

"Well, what are we waiting for?" demanded Mee-maw, already rummaging in her bag.

"What are you doing?" Patrick asked, holding an arm out. "We can't just use the compass in front of everyone."

"You know, hotshot, that's actually a good point," Mee-maw acknowledged, and together we began to creep towards the display. "I'll just take a quick peek," she added. "Did you work out the kinks in your copycat potion yet, Zoe?"

"Not yet," Zoe replied, "but I'm close."

We had to assume Ethan would realize pretty quickly that something was missing later that night when he packed up his offerings. And, while arguably the item belonged to Mee-maw and wasn't technically being stolen, we still felt compelled to make it right with him. The plan was to make a duplicate of Mee-maw's item once we had it in hand, and then have Trudy tell Ethan she found it in the library a few days after the exhibition cleanup.

"Close to what?" The sound of a new, all-too familiar voice

nearly made me groan, and I slowly turned around to see Marilee Rasmusson approaching us at mach speed.

"Nothing," Zoe and I replied in unison.

"Ooh, okay," she said, her tone turning conspiratorial, "I get it. Top secret. Is it about the..." Glancing around, she leaned forward and whispered, "Is it about the cult?"

We all stared at her blankly.

"Relax, it's okay!" Marilee cried. "Mitch told me everything. He said something about human sacrifice? Scary stuff!"

"Marilee," Zoe said, turning to her, "isn't it against the law for your husband to be talking about active cases?"

"Oh, silly Zoe," Marilee replied, her voice saccharine as she trilled a laugh. "That's only for doctors and priests. Besides, the case won't be active after today, anyway."

"Listen, Marilee, now isn't really a good time," I told her, my patience wearing thin. "How about we catch up later?"

"No problem, I'm sure you've got your mind on other things than silly old me. Good luck with the cult!"

She said it loud enough to garner a few curious stares, which I ignored.

As soon as she had sauntered away, I turned back to the others. "Well?" I asked Mee-maw. "Do you sense anything? I'd really like to get out of here before she can corner me like that again."

Mee-maw nodded. "Actually, I think so," she replied, pausing to glance into her bag where the compass was. "I think it's at that table over there," she said, jerking her head towards the display closest to the exit.

"Good," Patrick said. "Let's grab it and get out of here. This place is making me uneasy. Too many people." But just as the words left his mouth, I stopped short and clutched his arm, my whole body going rigid.

A familiar-looking man stood in the doorway dressed in a dark suit, rocking a pair of black gloves and sunglasses.

Crap.

"Cricket?" Patrick asked, looking down at me. "What's...?" He followed my gaze.

"Is that...?" Zoe asked, leaning in.

Patrick gave her a grim nod. "Yup. They either followed us in the Uber, or sent him out on a hunch when they heard about the exhibit. Let's just hope he's alone."

"What do we do now?" Zoe hissed.

"We do exactly what we were going to do," Patrick replied. "But instead of taking the item with us when we leave, we're going to hide it in the basement and have Trudy get it for us later. They're definitely going to tail us on the way home, and if there's another confrontation, we can't risk letting them get their hands on it. Let's hurry before he can call for backup, though."

I turned to glance at the door again, and then blinked.

He was gone.

Frantic, I stood on my tiptoes, trying to catch sight of him again over the sea of people, but it was no use—he was gone.

And somehow, that was even scarier than if he had stayed.

What were they up to?

I wasn't sure, but things just got a lot more complicated.

CHAPTER 20

"Something isn't right. I know you always say they won't make a move with civilians around, Patrick, but I've got a bad feeling. We've got to get out of here before we put all these people in danger," I whispered as a chill ran over me, so strong that my hands began to shake.

No one argued with me.

I'd barely taken hold of Mee-maw's arm when the library doors burst open again.

"Get on the floor, shut up and keep your hands where I can see them!" a voice shouted. "Nobody moves, nobody gets hurt."

Two men in black ski masks brandishing pistols strided in, making a show of aggression by roughly throwing a nearby man to the ground.

Too late.

I dropped to the floor, pulse hammering as I pulled Mee-maw down beside me as gently as possible.

And icy resignation settled over me as I considered my options, which seemed to have run dry. I couldn't use my magic in such a public place. Especially when doing so would almost certainly have them firing those pistols if I didn't manage to take them down.

My magic was getting stronger, but I still didn't have the kind of control that left me confident enough to wager the lives of innocent people on it.

"I said get down!" the man repeated, aiming the weapon into the crowd.

I heard a thud beside me as Patrick dropped and slung a protective arm around my shoulder.

At least we were all together.

I turned my head to the side, watching the "robbers" step carefully through the crowd, one man grabbing items from the displays and shoving them into four massive duffel bags while the other stood a few feet away, pointing his gun at anyone who shifted or seemed like they might try something. The process took all of five minutes, the entirety of which I spent wracking my brain for a good solution to our latest problem.

I cringed as they began making their way over to us, one of the men seemingly aiming his pistol directly at me.

Were they planning to use this as an opportunity to kidnap me and steal the object in one go? Would they really risk taking me in front of dozens of people?

It would be a bold move. One that would likely result in a lot of headaches for the Organization, but they were clearly getting desperate.

That caused a whole other anxiety. I feared what the others in my group might do if they tried to take me as much as my own kidnapping; would they try to stop them and get killed in the process?

Mee-maw and Zoe were too valuable to kill, but what about Patrick, Trudy, and Ethan? If the Organization decided to surrender the facade of only harming witches, they were all expendable.

As the thoughts raced through my head, though, they stepped right by me, to the objects on the table closest to us.

"They won't risk it," Patrick whispered, inches away from my ear.

I flinched, startled, and realized that I'd been shaking like a leaf. Hopefully, he was right. He *had* been one of them, after all, and he probably knew how they thought a heck of a lot better than I did.

Sure enough, once they cleared off the final table, they made their way directly toward the door. I cringed as I heard a rustling sound next to me and found Mee-maw fumbling through her purse. "Stop!" I hissed. "Let it go."

She struggled for a moment longer before going limp with resignation. "I'm going to pop a cap in those bastards one of these days," she vowed, her tone lethal.

For a long moment after the doors closed behind them, everyone remained motionless. A few seconds later, the low drone of chatter began.

"Is everyone okay?" Ethan was calling to the room in general as he helped Trudy to her feet and moved to help the older women closest to them.

There were murmured yeses as everyone slowly stood, with a mix of bewilderment and anger on their faces.

I stood, helping my grandmother up, before making my way over to Ethan and Trudy, along with Patrick and Zoe, who was already on the phone with the 911 operator.

"Are you guys okay?" I asked. But, of course, they weren't. Not really. Trudy's cheeks were chalky and Ethan looked stricken and distraught.

"We weren't hurt," Ethan said with a clipped nod. "You guys?"

Understanding dawned as he shot a glance to Patrick's hand, which was on the small of my back. A spike of guilt shot through me at the hurt in his eyes. Ethan really was a good man and it was a kick in the gut to know that I'd hurt him, but if I'd ever imagined a world in which we ended up together, the dream had been truly shattered today.

He'd never had to witness the darkness that inhabited the earth. Who was I to steal that from him? Ethan deserved something lovely. Something easy.

And me? I was a walking nuclear bomb. Hitching a wagon to me was tantamount to hitching up to a pack of dragons. This wasn't how I'd wanted to tell him, but the results were the same, regardless.

There would never be an Ethan and me. My life was way too complicated for normal, now. Assuming I even made it past next week...

I shook myself out of that line of thinking as Trudy sidled closer to me. We had other things to deal with right now, I'd make things right once we handled things with the Organization.

"That was really stupid," Trudy said, wearing her stern librarian face as she glared at Ethan. "You've got a little problem with impulse control, don't you?"

He blinked at her. "I--"

"Nobody needs a dead hero, Ethan," she said waspishly before turning to the rest of us. "I had to practically hold him down when they were taking the stuff. Things are replaceable. People aren't," she said, her eyes going suspiciously shiny.

"Some of those items were one of a kind, so not really. But I'll get over the artifacts. One of those guys looked twitchy to me. I was afraid he was going to shoot someone," Ethan admitted with a shrug. "We got through it unscathed, and I'm so grateful."

"So what now?" Patrick asked smoothly. "The police are on their way, but Mrs. Hawthorne isn't feeling well, and I don't think it's a good idea to put her through even more stress."

Mee-maw opened her mouth to protest, but clearly thought better of it at a pointed glance from Patrick. "Yeah. I'm feeling a fit of the vapors coming on," she said gruffly, holding a hand to her forehead like a mullet-sporting Scarlett O'Hara.

Trudy nodded. "Ethan and I will handle the cops. You guys go ahead and call the Uber."

Ethan made a confused face, cocking his head at me. "You didn't bring a car?"

I opened my mouth to make some excuse but luckily, Zoe walked back over, saving me the trouble. "They're on their way, shouldn't be too long and they'll be taking statements from as many witnesses as they can once they get here."

"We have to get Mee-maw home," I said, pointedly meeting Zoe's eyes as I continued, "she's feeling weak, I think she might be having one of her episodes."

Mee-maw grumbled, squeezing my arm with displeasure, but said nothing.

"Yeah, we'd better," Zoe said, herding us quickly toward the door before Ethan could ask any more questions.

It was a short and blessedly uneventful ride home, though Mee-maw had spent half of it letting me know exactly how annoyed she was at being treated like some ancient relic in need of protection. The adrenaline had left my body and I was no longer freaking out, but the situation seemed to be a hell of a lot more dire than it'd been less than an hour earlier.

One moment, we'd been just about to put the entire coven back together with Mee-maw's item within arm's reach *again*, and the next, we were back to square one. At least nobody had been hurt, or worse.

"Why were you so sure they wouldn't nab us, or at least me?" I asked, plopping down next to Patrick on the office floor of the bakery.

"People were willing to put their hands up and lay on the floor for a robbery, but surely there would be a good number who would balk at letting two gunmen drag a woman out right in front of them," he added. "Plus, the cop guarding the bakery every night is a pretty clear sign that we've already spoken to the police. One of us being kidnapped in public would've added a lot more credibility to whatever we told them to get them involved in the first place. Most importantly, though, like the prophecy said, they like the cover of darkness. It's a covert operation. Risking civilian lives in public is reckless. I don't hold any delusions that they care who they hurt. Not anymore, at least. But the less scrutiny they're under, the better. That means no human casualties if they can help it. Taking you could've triggered a violent encounter."

I nodded slowly. That made sense, too, and actually went a long way to soothing my immediate concerns for Lizzie and Jack. So far, the Organization had kept their sights firmly on me and my coven. They'd only burned Greg's house down because I'd been there, and they wanted to scare me. If they'd wanted to hurt him or the kids, they would've.

I paused a long time before continuing, my voice cracking as I spoke. "We were so *freaking* close. We only had one more table to look over when they came, and Mee-maw was just beginning to sense her item." I clenched my fist tight, feeling hopeless. Maybe we could've come up with a better plan if I hadn't been in such a rush.

"Don't count us out yet," Mee-maw said, rummaging in her bag.

"What do you mean?" Zoe asked.

"Look!" Mee-maw said, pulling out her delicate golden compass and opening it. The needle was moving slowly to the right as I watched. "They don't know about this bad boy, right? Which means, they're basically going to lead us straight to their lair!"

I stared at the compass for a long moment, stunned that I hadn't thought of that, but afraid to let myself rejoice just yet. "Patrick, has the Organization ever seen something like our compasses in the past?"

"Not to my knowledge," Patrick said, shaking his head, "and my father will almost certainly want the items they just stole close by so he can keep an eye on them personally. The compass will almost certainly lead us to him."

Could this awful turn of events actually wind up being the best thing that could've happened to us? My mind went back to my partially completed prophecy...If time was ticking, having a path straight to the heart of the Organization and Finneas could speed up our plans considerably. Especially when we'd have the element of surprise on our side.

"There's still the problem of how we can actually face them all at once. My father is a cautious man and I've rarely seen him without at least a dozen armed guards around him."

"What if we lure them away?" Zoe said.

I cocked my head. "What do you have in mind?"

"Well, I spent most of the day yesterday working on a new idea I came up with as I was working on my copycat potion," Zoe said, "and I made a breakthrough in the middle of the night with a batch of lemon bars. So far, they only last a couple hours, but I can work out that kink in the next batch." She let out a breath and then grinned. "Eating one allows you to take on the appearance of another person, so long as you're looking at them when you eat it. I'm calling it the doppelganger."

She dropped that on us like it wasn't a bomb.

"Are you kidding, Zoe?" I demanded. "That's amazing. Holy crap." Her powers had ramped up so much more quickly than mine. Although, she did have the benefit of knowing what was happening to her and leaning into it, as opposed to spending the first couple weeks of her new adventure wondering if she hadn't lost her mind.

"That's pretty amazing," Patrick said, leaning forward with more enthusiasm than he'd ever shown about magic, albeit tempered by caution. "What exactly is the plan, though?"

Zoe nodded, holding her head high with pride. "Well, I don't have it all detailed out yet because I hadn't thought about the compass leading us straight to them. With that in mind, I'm thinking that the Organization showed that they're willing to take direct action against us when they went after us at the cemetery, right? They also found out how powerful Cricket is and won't be likely to send such a small crew after her next time. They need a lot of firepower to take us down now. Why don't we use that against them? What if one of us disguises ourselves as Cricket, as a decoy, to draw the bulk of the muscle away, while the rest of us use Mee-maw's compass to locate their Rocky Knoll headquarters and attack Finneas and those left to guard him? If we get Finneas, the whole thing crumbles, right? The head of the snake, and all..."

"It would certainly weaken them immensely," Patrick acknowledged carefully.

"And then we can also get my item!" Mee-maw added.

"But who is going to pretend to be me? It sounds dangerous."

"Not as dangerous as you'd think," Zoe said. "If what they did last time is anything to go by, they have a whole ritual they need to complete before they can kill you, so we'd have a window. Especially if they wait until midnight like last time.

We can time the change back to normal so that they'd know we tricked them before they executed the wrong person." She lifted her chin and eyed us all stubbornly. "Which makes me the best choice. Mee-maw needs to be on site with you to connect with her item, and I'm the only other one of us with a presumption of safety. They don't want me hurt until I've fully charged my cauldron with power. They have no idea how strong I've become already. It's got to be me."

"Or me," Patrick interjected. "Although, I don't like the idea of you all fighting the Organization without me, either..."

The person walking into the Organization's clutches would be at risk, no matter what either of them said. They might not die, but there were things worse than dying...

I shook my head, opening my mouth to speak, but Zoe cut me off.

"Look, let's not be hasty. It's dark out already. We'll get some rest, think it through, and talk about it in the morning. I'll try another batch before I go to bed that will hopefully lengthen the effects by a third, and we can test them tomorrow. I'm *exhausted,*" Zoe said, shaking her head sadly. "I think everyone will do better after a good night of rest and a day of preparation, anyway."

I knew she was right, but I also knew that—like Maude said—the clock was ticking. That deep, ever-growing ember of magic in my belly felt it now, like a steadily increasing heartbeat.

Something needed to happen, and fast. Our very lives depended on it.

CHAPTER 21

I WOKE up in a pool of sweat, my whole body as hot as a furnace. Careful not to wake Patrick as I disengaged from his embrace, I pressed the button on my cell phone.

Only five thirty in the morning but there was no way I'd be able to sleep through all this heat and, unlike a regular hot flash, it wouldn't just pass with time.

Typing on Maude was the only way I'd get rid of this horrible feeling inside me, and I was thankful for it. Despite all the magic flying around at the bakery lately, I hadn't made a single prediction in days and I was desperate for some guidance before carrying out our bold plan later in the day.

I padded quietly past Mee-maw and Zoe, avoiding the creaky board in the middle of the room even in the darkness, and grabbed Maude from the desk before slipping out the door and into the bakery storefront room.

I set Maude on the table and pushed my hair back, allowing myself to enter the trance-like state that came along with my predictions. The words came, fast and furious, without prompting or delay. A few minutes later, I left the fugue state, feeling like I'd just woken up for the second time in the day, though at least this time I didn't feel like I was about to combust.

I held my breath as I glanced down at the paper in front of me.

While the plan to lure the enemy from their nest and strike at their leader is sound, the cost of victory will be high and one of your comrades will never return. Though the possibility of failure is greater, you will have to enter the belly of the beast alone to have any chance of your numbers remaining whole. Choose wisely, for still-greater challenges await you.

My breath caught in my throat as I stared at the words until they blurred in front of me.

This was bad. The plan we'd hatched could result in someone I loved being killed. But, if I went alone, I faced a greater chance of failing, which might see us all dead in the long run.

This was a critical decision. Making the wrong one could haunt me for the rest of my life, however long or short it might be. And still, it was one I made easily.

I couldn't sacrifice anyone in my group—I wouldn't—no matter the price. I'd rather be dead than live with that on my conscience. I needed to take this golden opportunity to take down Finneas, and I needed to do it solo.

I pulled the paper out and sat still, reading and re-reading, for a long while, making sure I didn't miss a single word or nuance. Without Mee-maw with me to activate her compass, it would be useless to me. And, even if I could find Finneas on my own, I couldn't exactly go waltzing in there. I'd get taken down instantly by a dozen male guards armed with weapons and magic, and find myself on the wrong end of a noose again.

Which meant there was only one viable option that would allow me to "enter the belly of the beast alone". One I relished about as much as the thought of sticking a rusty fork in my eye, but my path was clear.

I nodded, feeling the weight of our mission resting on my shoulders in a way that was strangely comforting. I pocketed the paper and padded to the refrigerator to snag one of Zoe's lemon bars. Then, I headed quietly back into the office and stood over the daybed where Mee-maw lay.

Her wrinkly face was relaxed in sleep, and I resisted the urge to lean down and kiss her cheek...just in case.

With a silent prayer, I shoved the bar into my mouth whole and chewed, sparing a glance at the clock.

After six. Mee-maw would be up no later than seven, and I'd have to be gone before then.

I spared sleeping Patrick and Zoe quick looks, silently saying my goodbyes before heading back into the kitchen.

Luckily, it didn't take long for the magic to kick in as I felt myself begin to shrink. My vision slowly blurred, my muscles grew soft and achy, my hip throbbed. Worst of all, my magic faded into the background, like a low, static hum just out of reach.

It was probably for the best. I would need to be back to myself—both physically and magically—before I made a move once in captivity. Mee-maw's body couldn't withstand the kind of battle I'd likely be facing. Not having easy access to my magic would keep me from drawing on it instinctively out of fear.

But, damn, did it leave me feeling vulnerable. Like an armadillo flat on its back.

When it was over, I pulled up my phone's camera, using it as a mirror and nodding in satisfaction at how much I looked like Mee-maw.

Zoe was an absolute genius. If I wasn't staring down the barrel of my own possible demise, I'd have been gobsmacked by the breadth, scope, and power of her witchery.

But I had work to do. For a few minutes, I practiced my gait and posture as I walked around the room, feeling like a newborn foal as I struggled to get used to the new body. Then, I changed from my now too-large clothes into Mee-maw's smaller ones.

I was halfway to the door when the enormity of what I was setting off to do hit me like a train.

I was going to fight a giant, international conglomerate of evil men with magic at their disposal *by myself* and there was a serious chance that I'd never make it back. The least I owed my family was some type of explanation in case they never saw me again.

I shuffled back inside, pulling the prophecy out of my pocket, and searching for a pen. I found one, after a few moments of looking, next to the cash register, and made my way back over to the prediction I'd just made, scribbling a short explanation of my plans onto the bottom of it:

I'm sorry, but I love you all too much and I won't risk any of you, even if it means putting the mission in jeopardy. I've gone to face the organization and to retrieve Mee-maw's item so we can make the coven whole. Don't try to follow me.

-Cricket

I folded the note and stuck it into the fridge, leaning it against the tray of lemon bars. I turned around, not giving myself time to think about whether it was a mistake or not, and walked out the door.

I'd kind of hoped it would happen fast. That I'd walk outside and someone would just snag me right in the parking lot, before the dread fully kicked in.

But that didn't happen. Instead, I had to hotfoot it all the way to Mee-maw's house. I was out of breath by the time I got there, though it was just a handful of blocks away. And I'd thought age had taken a toll on *my* body?

I took a few deep breaths as I ambled up to the walkway, trying to resist the urge to look around for the Organization member that would no doubt be watching the house. I made it all the way to the stoop, untouched, though. Trying to act natural, I let myself into the house using the key under the mat, trying not to flinch away from the blow that would surely come.

But again, nothing.

Had I been wrong? Had they given up watching 24/7 now that they knew we'd set up camp in the bakery?

I had trudged into the entryway and was setting the key down when I heard it.

Footsteps.

I slapped the sides of my face, forcing myself to focus as I padded into the kitchen on creaky knees. I *was* capable of this. In order to keep them from suspecting anything, I'd have to put on a good show. I grabbed a broom from the corner of the room and raised it, facing the door.

Seconds later, a man in a black ski mask charged in, raising a pistol. I swung the broomstick at him, striking him in the face as I shouted with rage. "Get the hell out of my house, you vagabond!"

He grabbed the broom and yanked it, and me, forward, grabbing me by the shoulders. A sense of relief washed over me as I struggled, thrashing violently, and uselessly, against his firm grip. I'd been expecting to take a few punches or kicks before they managed to subdue me, but this was much easier.

"Let me go!" I yelled.

"Stop struggling and you won't be harmed, old woman," the man muttered.

I'd assumed they wouldn't simply kill Mee-maw without

waiting for her to bond with a magical item that they could steal from her, but it was music to my ears to hear that I was right.

"Stay still, damn it," he commanded, sounding almost sorry for me as he duct-taped my wrists and ankles together.

"Help!" I screamed, hoping he wouldn't hit me. I couldn't give them any reason to doubt that I was who I seemed to be, and nobody would just give up on trying to escape when being kidnapped.

"Be quiet," he said, stretching out another piece of duct tape and wrapping it around my mouth. He laid me on the ground and pulled out his phone. The call didn't take long, he just explained the situation and asked for them to send a car. I did my best to keep my mind on the plan and off the panic caused by the bonds while we waited. It felt like an eternity later when his phone rang again.

"Copy that, headed outside now." He threw me over his shoulder and tossed a blanket on top of me to hide what he was carrying as he made his way back through the house.

Every fiber of my being was screaming at me to try and use my magic to escape as I struggled and writhed, partially for show and partially with real fear. As he pulled open the car's door a moment later, though, no acting was needed.

"Good work," a gravelly voice said from the front seat as he tossed me into the back, "we should be able to use this one to lure the clairvoyant in, no problem. Can't wait to get my hands on that witch."

A cold sweat broke out on my neck as my captor, who now sat next to me, pulled the blanket away from my face. What I'd already suspected was affirmed as I stared at the man in front of me, unable to take my eyes away from the jagged cut on his right cheek.

A wound *I* had made.

It was the Organization's jailor, who had tortured me

beyond what I'd thought possible with the horrible magical item he wore around his neck and haunted my dreams.

"Hello, Granny," he said, nodding before turning back to his partner. "We'll have this damned coven stamped out by the end of the month. I'll put in a good word for you with the bossman, but you'd better stay behind. The rest of them might come looking for their granny and we'll have ourselves a trifecta."

I was almost thankful as the person in the back seat pulled the blanket back over my face, obscuring my view of the man in front of me.

I spent the rest of the car ride in a panic, trying to catch my breath. For some reason, I thought I'd mentally prepared myself for this eventuality. I'd even ran through a number of scenarios in my head about how I'd keep myself calm with mantras and affirmations.

But the reality was far different than my imaginings, and while my body had healed, my mind was still a bit broken from what I'd suffered.

The fact was that I'd never gone through anything as hideously painful as I had at that moment. I'd rather have experienced the pain of giving birth for a hundred hours than feel even one second of the agony from that demon necklace, yet I had dropped myself right back into his hands and at his mercy. There was no turning back now.

I flinched as the car lurched to a stop and the front door clicked open.

"We're here!" Necklace said cheerily, opening my door. A shudder of revulsion rolled over me as he grabbed me and tossed me over his shoulder. "Don't worry, Granny. You'll be nice and comfortable soon enough."

Despite his encouraging words, as he walked with his necklace jingling with each step, I could barely keep my bladder from emptying. If he again became my guard, how could I possibly defeat him to even get a shot at Finneas? I could barely keep from peeing myself, never mind beat him in a battle of magic.

As fear tightened its stranglehold on me, the cold hard facts became clear, almost breaking me completely right then and there.

The second Zoe's doppelganger magic gave out, this man was going to torture me in the most hideous fashion possible.

And there was nothing I could do about it.

CHAPTER 22

"You know, I don't usually let myself get all worked up about ridding the world of witches like Finneas and the others, glassy-eyed, with the chanting and all that garbage," Necklace said, grinning coldly, "but that granddaughter of yours has me really fired up. This old face of mine wasn't all that hot to begin with, but things are going to get a lot tougher with the ladies after what she did to me." He pointed at the sloppily stitched gash on his cheek with his index finger.

"Not to mention, getting me into trouble with the boss. We've got some squaring up to do, her and I."

I'd been locked up in a makeshift cell that actually looked like some sort of storage room in an office building for the past ten minutes with him, but this was the first time he'd spoked to me since we'd arrived. Before that, he'd been busy tapping away on his phone, probably in contact with other members of the Organization. It had given me a little much-needed time to pull myself together, but I was still hanging on by a string.

Now, he'd set the device aside to give me his full attention. Apparently, he was in the mood to chat.

Lucky me.

Still, if chatter was what he wanted, that was what I'd give him, in hopes that he'd get his fill of me—or Mee-maw, to his mind—and go away for a few minutes. It was only a matter of time until I turned back and, as I'd never taken this potion before, I didn't have a good gauge of how vulnerable I'd be during the transition or how long it would take.

"Why do this, if not for the witches?" I replied in Mee-maw's voice, which was still rather jarring.

He stared at me pensively for a long moment before answering my question. "I guess it's about the power. If someone's gotta have it, it might as well be me, no?"

No.

"After you have your fun and your boss kills my granddaughter, what happens next?" I rasped, not allowing myself to fall apart again as I stared back at him.

My breath caught in my throat as I realized that somewhat-blurred vision was clearing, ever so slightly, and the aching in my bones began to fade. I reached tentatively for my magic, but it still felt like trying to grab a handful of mist or smoke from the air, dispersing and scattering every time I tugged for it.

"Worried about your own hide, eh?" he said, smiling. "I can respect that. First, we'll let the cousin develop more so we can take her magical item. And then we'll give you yours, Granny. I'm not sure on the time frame at your age. Could take longer for you to charge yours, so you might be able to make it a few months. Better get to work on that bucket list." His phone beeped and he looked down, cocking his head as he read a message.

A deep chill ran through me as I considered what he'd said. How could I give up trying when the rest of my family would be next? My racing thoughts slowed to a near stop as I noticed that my line of sight was rising ever so slightly, as if I was growing. Still crippled by fear, I reached back into my well of magic, grabbing at any of the wisps I could get my hands on, using thoughts of my family for strength as I willed it not to dissipate.

He set his phone aside and I knew it was now or never. I took the meager scraps of power I'd gathered and *pushed* with all I had. Necklace shot off his feet like he'd been popped by an unseen sniper and landed flat on his back.

Unfortunately, the blast had been impotent and I was still in limbo between my own form and Mee-maw's. Aside from having the wind knocked out of him, my captor hardly even seemed fazed as he got back to his feet.

"Well, hot damn," he muttered. "You wily little so and so. It was you the whole time?" He grinned, a cold smile that didn't reach his eyes.

I shuddered as he reached for the chain around his neck, pushing all thoughts of fear from my mind. There was no way I could allow this man to beat me. I dug deep for my magic again, finally feeling like myself as it came bubbling closer to the surface, but he was faster.

The pain, like a thousand unimaginable tortures all at once, gripped me in its clutches and my brain went offline even as my body convulsed. It was somehow more than the simple experience of pain, as if my entire consciousness had *become* agony itself.

"You should've just went down easily the first time. You brought this on yourself."

I could hear the words perfectly fine but my brain was slow to parse them into any kind of sense as I tried not to go insane in my agony.

"I've always wondered what that feels like," he said, stepping closer to me. "I guess I'll have to ask your cousin and granny when I use it on them, huh? Think of how much easier things could've been for all three of you if you weren't so stubborn."

After a long moment of struggling to decipher his words, a fiery anger rose inside of me. I couldn't just resign to the pain if this man was going to torture Zoe and Mee-maw as a result of something *I* had done. I had to figure out a way to fight. With images of my coven, Patrick and Trudy included, shimmering in my mind like a beacon, I pried at the door to my magic once again, forcing it to come out rather than simply reaching for it.

I would not allow it to refuse me.

Suddenly, a great wave of light came streaming through me, not overtaking the pain, but keeping it at bay. If one half of my experience was pure pain, the other was filled with an overwhelming calmness and serenity.

With every ounce of will I had left, I pressed against the blinding pain, tamping it down even further, and finding my center once again. The pain was still there, lurking like a specter, but I could bear it.

I *would* bear it.

I forced my head up, meeting Necklace's eyes.

"What happened?" he said, looking down at his necklace, his face contorted with terror.

I called on the huge reservoir of power, which had only grown since I'd used it last, and attacked. With one sweep of my hand, I lifted his body into the air, twisting it as my own pain faded away, leaving behind a sweet relief.

Necklace raised an arm, screaming for me to stop. For a moment, I was filled with a vengeful hatred, wanting to go even further in my assault on him, but held back. Unlike him, I took no true pleasure in causing pain. I released him in one fell swoop, dropping him to the ground in a heap, before blasting my cell door off of its hinges with a thought and walking toward him.

"How?" he managed, barely able to speak through a blubbering fit of snot and tears.

"You're a petty man doing his best impression of a witch. I'm the real thing," I said, shoving back my revulsion to grab his necklace and snap it off with a rough tug.

I ignored his shouts as I rushed out through the door leading out of the room. Judging by the unnatural angle of his ankle, he wouldn't be following me anytime soon, and, unlike the Organization, I wasn't into cold-blooded murder.

As I stepped into the hallway, I headed left, which was the opposite way from where we'd come in. My mind went back to the two times I'd felt the pain that the necklace could cause. Now, as I looked at its beautiful, delicate design, my crippling fear of the thing was gone. I had overcome it and things were different now.

I was different now.

I was drawn away from my thoughts at a strange alarm sound in the distance, like some kind of warning system. Had Necklace triggered some kind of alarm to signal my escape? I didn't have much time to think it over as a man came charging down the hallway, a pistol on his hip and a radio pulled close to his face.

He jumped as he saw me, reaching for his gun, but I was faster, throwing him to the wall with a sickening thud. I walked up to him, hoping I hadn't overdone it, and was happy to find that he was still breathing. "Don't come after me and you'll be fine."

"Damned witch," he spat, pulling a knife from his belt with his unbroken left arm and stabbing toward me with it.

I blasted at him again, sending the weapon flying down the hall. "I'll be taking these," I said, pulling his gun from his holster and the walkie talkie from his combat vest. He struggled halfheartedly against me but he was in no state to resist.

I stepped back, shaking my head as he cursed me, and clipped the walkie talkie to my shirt. "There has been a breach in the perimeter," a crackly voice said through the radio, "I repeat, there has been a breach."

I cocked my head, wondering what they meant by a breach. Where were we and who would want to attack the Organization directly? Could it be the police? It all snapped into place as the next transmission came through.

"All units, be advised that the intruders have been identified as two witches from the Crow's Feet Coven and the Traitor himself. All hands on deck!"

The Crow's Feet Coven?

That was us. Mee-maw, Patrick, and Zoe were here.

A shot of terror-laden adrenaline pumped through me as I broke into a run.

In my headlong rush into near-certain martyrdom, I had forgotten about the compass. If I'd taken it, they couldn't have followed me.

It was too late to cry over that puddle of milk now, though. I had to find Finneas and take him out, and quickly, before they got themselves hurt, or worse. I barreled down the hallway, turning left when I had to, and gulped as I realized that the hallway didn't have any more turns. There was one door at the end that was different from the others, made of thick steel with no window.

Having no time to spare for stealth, I called on my magic and slammed it forward, denting the door inward and bashing it off of its hinges as if it was made of aluminum foil.

I sped into the open room in front of me to find high ceilings and a single wooden door in the back with two guards standing in front of it.

"Stop her, even if you have to kill her!" a voice came from the room behind them, cracking with fear.

I pulled my hand back, ready to send out a blast of magic,

when a smattering of bullets whizzed by me, burrowing into the wall just behind me.

Way too close.

I straightened and flicked my wrist, sending the guards sailing into the door behind them in two crumpled piles. One let out a pained cry before dropping to the ground, and the other was silent, but I didn't have time to worry whether I'd wounded him mortally or not when Finneas could be escaping.

I opened the next door, using magic to blast the lock, but, other than furniture and some shelves stacked with bric-a-brac and boxes, it was empty. Out of the corner of my eye, I caught sight of an open window and sprinted toward it, heart hammering.

"Finneas!" I shouted, my voice guttural and deep, a furious rage rising in me as I thought of all the witches that his people had murdered in the past and how Mee-maw, Zoe, and I could've been just like them.

I shimmied through the window, landing in what looked like a small courtyard, right as a *kaboom* sounded and a jolt of pain shot down my right leg. I looked up to see our greatest enemy, the leader of the Organization, standing just a few dozen feet away, a rifle pulled against his shoulder.

"I guess it's about time we end this, then," he said, shaking his head as he readied himself for another shot.

CHAPTER 23

THE HAZE of adrenaline powering me was the only thing keeping me from doubling over at the pain in my leg, but it still felt like someone had plunged a knife into my thigh. My body buzzed with magic, determination, and yes, fear, and for a brief, terrifying moment, I stood there paralyzed, staring down the barrel of Finneas's gun.

The shock of being face-to-face with the man who had already tried to kill me once was quickly overshadowed by the knowledge that he was about to try again. I managed to get my legs working a split second before another shot rang out in the courtyard, but his aim was good, and I wasn't quite fast enough.

I let out a hiss as the bullet pierced my left arm, bringing another surge of pain with it. Glancing down at the wound was a mistake, and I couldn't help but cry out when I saw the hole, which was already gushing dark red blood.

You're going to wind up with more holes than a colander if you don't shape up, I thought frantically as I made a mad dash toward the section of the courtyard lined with bushes, trees, and dilapidated benches.

Not the best as far as cover went, but I only had so much to work with.

A hot, red spot was staining my pants—I was losing blood, along with my focus.

Another shot ricocheted off the stone wall behind me, sending fragments of rock raining down on top of me. I wasn't liking all these close calls. Now that I had a little protection, it was time to turn the tables and get on the offensive. Whirling around, I reached for the reserve of magic I had been tapping and let out a manic blast of energy, but lifting my arm was a mistake; the pain was almost enough to knock me off my feet, and I wavered, causing me to miss Finneas completely. The charge of power hit a nearby shrub, sending leaves exploding into the air on a puff of wasted energy.

"Stop," he demanded, training his gun on me once more. "It's over, Cricket."

I longed to make a snarky reply, like a movie action hero, but the pain was too much for me to do anything other than grit my teeth and summon my magic again. I was losing control of it— like it was getting away from me, and I was helpless to stop it.

Not good.

Finneas shot at me again, and I used my good arm to let out another pulse of energy. It was enough to knock the bullet off its course, but my energy was flagging, and I knew it.

From the looks of it, Finneas knew it, too, but he needed to reload. Time to act.

Groaning with the effort, I crouched low in the bushes. My limbs were starting to feel like jelly, and there was a ringing in my ears; he must have hit an artery, which was bad news for me. I couldn't help dropping to my knees behind the thicket as my injured leg finally gave out. "You really want to make this difficult, don't you?" Finneas called, hoisting up his rifle again. He was hunting me like an animal, and he had me backed into a corner. "Fine," he said when I didn't respond. "Have it your way."

I lurched out of the way, pushing another pulse of magic in his direction just as he shot at me again, but my aim was only getting worse the more blood I lost. My shirt was already soaked with it, and the world was starting to spin around me. I bit my lip—it was all I could do to keep from passing out—and tried to summon another spell, but it was no use. I was losing my grip on my magic. The dizziness worsening, the world felt like it was going to close in on me at any second.

Frantic, I fumbled for something, anything, that might stop him—or at least delay the inevitable...and then my fingers closed around the amulet in my pocket. Gingerly, I pulled it out and examined it. It radiated a dark energy, and just looking at it made me feel sick to my stomach, but there was no time to get squeamish. Finneas was lining up another shot, and he was aiming right between my eyes. Digging deep, I scrambled for the last remnants of my energy, channeling it into the amulet before raising it in one last, desperate gesture.

Finneas stopped dead in his tracks, as if he'd been struck by lightning, and then the rifle clattered to the ground. He let out a gut-wrenching cry of pain, dropping to his knees and wrapping his arms around himself as the pain coursed through him, rocking his body. His eyes clamped shut, and he yelled out again: "Please...make it stop!"

I grunted, sitting up a little straighter as I continued to force my remaining power into the amulet. It felt bad, using a dead witch's magic—especially magic this destructive—but I knew that if the shoe were on the other foot, I would want my sisters to do the same with mine if it meant saving their lives and the lives of their covens.

"Please!" Finneas cried again, his voice hoarse. "You got me, all right? Just...please...no more..." His words subsided into tortured moans, and I was surprised to find myself feeling a pang of sympathy for the man. I knew what this amulet did to a person. He just suddenly seemed so utterly broken. And something in Finneas's voice told me that, in spite of it all, he was sincere...about this, at least. I put on the brakes as best as I could, pulling the magic back out of the amulet and lowering my hand, which was shaking from the pain and the effort.

The world was still going fuzzy around me but I remained on guard and ready to fire again as he sat there panting for a long moment, his eyes wide and staring, before he slowly struggled to sit up, cradling his head in his hands.

"Cricket!" The sound of Patrick's voice was enough to pull me back from the brink, like something from a dream. How on earth...? I looked up to see him, Mee-maw and Zoe charging out of a side door and into the courtyard, metaphorical guns blazing —literal guns blazing in the case of Mee-maw, who had her pistol drawn and at the ready, like something out of James Bond. Zoe and Mee-maw rushed to me, and I could only look up at them as they dropped to the ground beside me.

"Bloody hell," Patrick said, putting a hand on my shoulder as Zoe and Mee-maw took in the sight of my injuries, "what happened?"

"Finneas shot me."

"I'll say," Mee-maw muttered, although I could hear the thinly-disguised panic in her voice. "He went full-on Rambo on you! But it looks like you're doing better than he is," she added, sparing a glance to a still-moaning Finneas a handful of yards away.

"I got a few good shots in," I countered. "What are you doing here?" I added, hissing as Zoe pulled my shirt sleeve away to examine my wound.

"We saw your note," Zoe explained. "We came to create a distraction."

"And when they came after us, Zoe managed to knock them out with a noxious potion she made into an aerosol. We knew you had to take Finneas on alone, so we figured we could at least keep the rest of them from making it any harder. And it looks like we were right to come," Mee-maw added, glancing down at my shot leg. "Your dad's a real piece of work," she informed Patrick.

As if remembering that his father was still on the other side of the courtyard, Patrick glanced over at Finneas, who had finally gone silent. For a long, tense moment, the two men just stared at one another until Patrick slowly got to his feet and walked over to him.

Fear shot through me as I watched. "Patrick--"

But he held up a staying hand as he approached his father. "Who are you?" he demanded, his voice breaking.

"Patrick," Finneas began, "listen--"

"No," Patrick snapped, shaking his head. "You lied to me. For years. You involved me in something I'd never have agreed to...you hurt people. You told me my mother didn't care about me." His voice was lethal and his hands were clenched into fists at his sides.

"I was afraid," Finneas confessed, looking his son in the eyes. "I know that's probably hard to believe right now, but it's the truth. It all started out as plain old fear of the unknown. I was scared of your mother, at first—for longer than I want to admit. Her powers were dangerous, and I worried what would happen if she turned on me—or god forbid, you. It was only after she had blossomed and truly came into her power that I...I..."

"You started to resent her," Patrick snarled.

"Yes," Finneas admitted. "Her strength made me feel weak and small. I wanted the woman I loved back, but that love turned into hate. I don't think I really even realized it was happening, at first. Once she left, it felt like she had abandoned us. I was so angry. I just wanted things to go back to the way they were...and I was willing to do anything to make that happen. So I joined the Organization, to find her. To force her to come back." He shook his head. "In hindsight, I should have realized that was exactly why she never did."

"It was you all along," Patrick breathed. "The whole time you told me she didn't care about us anymore, you were the reason she was afraid to come back."

Finneas swallowed hard, his eyes filling with tears. "When you were young, yes. For what it's worth, Patrick, she loved you more than anything. And if she could have come back into your life once you grew up and left home, she would have."

Even through the pain and lethargy from the lost blood, the full meaning of his words hit me like a punch to the gut. One look at Patrick was enough to tell me he had understood, too, and I watched as his expression shifted from one of confusion to one of horror.

"She's dead," he said. It wasn't a question.

Finneas dropped his head and began to weep, his body shaking with shame and despair. "Yes," he said through his sobs. "The Organization located her decades ago. By then, I was so full of rage and wrapped up in my own feelings of betrayal that something inside me had snapped. In order to rationalize what I had done, I had to convince myself that witches were craven creatures of the devil and it was my job to ensure they were exterminated." He lifted his gaze back to his son, who was looking at him as if he'd never met the man in his life. "The second I stopped, it would mean facing myself—and what I had done." He took a shaky breath. "It would mean admitting that I was a monster."

"You are," Patrick said, his voice wracked with a mix of pain and rage.

"I deserve that," Finneas replied. "But by the time I truly looked within and realized what I'd become, it was too late. I was already at the mercy of someone much stronger than me."

Patrick's brow furrowed, and Mee-maw, Zoe, and I exchanged a look. "What are you talking about?" Patrick demanded.

"I was wrong to persecute them. I will own that. But you need to understand...Not all witches are good, son," Finneas said, shaking his head. "Some are the kind that made the Organization fearful of magic in the first place."

"No more lies," Zoe snapped, getting to her feet and taking a step towards the men. "Haven't you blamed witches enough?"

Finneas shook his head and swallowed audibly, suddenly struggling to catch his breath. "I wish I was lying. She's evil incarnate."

"Who?" I asked, my voice coming out as a croak.

Finneas faced me, his expression strained. "The witch who has been splitting her time between controlling your coven's Everlasting Conservator and me. V--" He began to hack, his mouth opening and closing and his jaw clenching as he fought to form the word. I realized with a surge of dread that this was exactly what had happened to Connie the last time we had seen her. Finneas grit his teeth, his whole body going tense as he struggled against the power of the spell. His barking cough intensified, the harsh grating sounds rocking his whole body as he choked out a single word.

"Verbena."

The word had barely left his lips when his body began to sizzle, his skin blistering and the moisture leaving his body in a cloud of steam. We could only watch in horror as he continued to shrink, his screams dying just before he collapsed to the ground as dry and leathery as a museum mummy.

My eyelids fluttered as I tried to process this all, even as darkness tried to drag me under. I was losing too much blood at the hands of Finneas Byrne for the second time. But when his mummified corpse sat upright and its mouth began moving like that of a macabre puppet, I managed to tune back in to my surroundings.

"So, sisters of the Crow's Feet Coven..." Finneas's cadaver said, its mouth opening and closing grotesquely like a marionette, "it looks like you've neutralized my favorite pawns. I wonder if you'll be as successful when you have to face the queen?"

With that, a shudder rolled through the shell that had been Patrick's father and, an instant later, a green light shot out of his mouth and into the sky, leaving the four of us staring after in stunned silence.

"Holy mackerel," Mee-maw whispered before turning toward me, her stunned expression changing to one of determination. "Zoe," she snapped. Coming to her senses, Zoe hurried to my side. "See if you can use your magic to help her heal," Mee-maw snapped, in full-on Warden-mode now. "I need to try to find my item before the guards get back." She dove into her purse in search of the compass.

Patrick, realizing the seriousness of my injuries, barely spared a second glance for his father before rushing to my side.

"Easy, Cricket, easy," he murmured, his grip on me warm and steadying. "Zoe..." he pleaded, face lined with fear as he looked at my cousin.

"I don't know what I can do, but I'll try!" Zoe said. She was already stripping off her jacket and wrapping it around my arm in a tourniquet while Patrick put pressure on my leg wound, his brow furrowed. "Hold still," she told me as she rested her hands on my shoulders. Moments later, I began to feel a warm, soothing energy flowing through me, as if she was transferring some of her own strength to me. It wasn't a quick fix by any means, but it was just enough that, within moments, the sharpest edge of the pain began to loosen its grip.

"The bleeding has slowed. We've got to get out of here before the guards come to and find us," Patrick muttered. He lifted me gently into his arms and headed in the direction that Mee-maw had gone, compass in hand. She scurried through a set of doors leading to the office where Finneas had climbed through the window. We were coming up behind her just in time to see her approaching a shelf near the back of the room.

A chill ran through me as she reached out with an unsteady hand to clutch something in her fist. Tears in her eyes and a triumphant look on her face, she turned around and held it out to us.

An elegant, gold pocket watch, as old as it was ornate.

One of Maude's most cryptic prophecies floated to my weary mind, and I shook my head in awe.

"That Verbena bitch better get her flying monkeys ready," Mee-maw said with a grin. "Time is ticking."

The End

Stay tuned for book three of the Crow's Feet Coven series, *Stealing Time***, out now and FREE in KU!**

If you loved **Brewing Trouble** but like a little steam in your paranormal romance, check out Christine's alter-ego, Chloe Cole and her Montana Dragons series, starting with **Coercion,** FREE with KU!

. . .

Forced to wed a dragon who wants her but will never love her...

When Willa Stone is cast aside by the alpha-wolf she's been promised to since birth, she's humiliated and angry, but also secretly relieved. Now, maybe she'll have the chance to mate for love. If her power-crazed parents will just give her a little time, she's sure to find the man of her dreams...

Dragon-shifter, Drake Blackbourne, has an itch to scratch and precious few options for an outlet. When the Stone family offers up their daughter's hand in exchange for protection and political favors, he agrees to wed her, sight unseen. Drastic times call for drastic measures and, so long as she does her part and keeps out of his way the rest of the time, surely he can manage to bed her, no matter how plain she might be.

What he doesn't expect is that captivating, defiant Willa will ignite a fire in him that will burn everything in its path, and turn both of their worlds upside down...

"I don't get it."

Greyson West sat up in his oversized desk chair and probed Willa's face with his laser-like gaze, but she managed not to react in spite of the tumult of emotions rioting inside her. When he reached out to touch her consciousness with his own, she shut down entirely, not ready or willing to let him in.

"What don't you 'get'?" Willa's mother asked, her chin raised at a haughtier angle than was appropriate when talking to her alpha.

There was no question that Grey took notice, but he kept his tone measured and polite as he turned his attention back her way. "Your fury seems out of line, Faustine. In fact, I had thought that we'd come to an agreement."

Her ramrod back went even straighter. "You fractured this pack with your abominable actions. Then you turned your back on your betrothal to our daughter and the ancient ways of our kind. I don't know what you expected to have happen, but this is what you've wrought, young man. I'm sure my husband and I will be the first of many elders taking a stand."

Grey's posture changed on a dime and his nostrils flared. Where he'd been open and almost apologetic before, now, he was flat out pissed.

Willa swallowed hard in an attempt to dislodge the golf ball that had been lodged in her throat for the past week.

She didn't love Grey. Never had, but, since birth, they were bonded. Sworn to one another by their families to mate and rule the pack together once Joseph, Grey's father, stepped down.

The whole stepping down thing hadn't come to pass, but Grey was now, indeed, the alpha. Only Willa wasn't by his side.

She shifted uncomfortably in her armchair and shot a quick glance toward Maggie, Grey's new mate who sat beside him.

She didn't hate the woman. Quite the contrary. From what Willa had seen and heard, she was tough, ballsy and seemed to be mad about Greyson. And Willa was glad for that. At least one of them had gotten to mate for love.

What was harder to swallow was the fact that Willa's entire identity had been tied up in this antiquated, now-broken, marriage deal. And now, even the wolves who considered themselves progressive and forward-thinking--the young generation who had sided with Grey to overthrow his tyrannical and murderous father--had turned their backs on her.

Where once, they'd treated her with a respect bordering on reverence, they now looked on her with pity. Whatever they might say with their mouths that made them come off as politically correct under this new regime, deep down, they thought she was damaged goods.

No two ways about it. She had lost her best friend and planned mate in one fell swoop, and she had no prospects. If the alpha had cast her aside, why would anyone else want her?

Raised voices caught her attention and she tore her gaze away from raven-haired, slim, Maggie right in time to see Grey turn his attention to her father.

"Jacob, come on now. Surely, you can see the time has come for change. Your ways...the old ways just don't work for us any longer. We need to co-exist with humans, not murder them. And the idea of arranged marriages in this day and age--"

"You entitled little pup," her father cut in, his face turning a mottled red. "Your father broke his back to build this pack. Now, you betray your entire bloodline by imprisoning him and taking over, and you think to pass judgment on me?" He tossed his head back and barked out a bitter laugh. "That's rich, Greyson."

He shoved himself to his feet, whipping his dark, wool coat over his shoulders as he did.

"Sit. Down," Grey commanded, his jaw clenched, and his silvery eyes blazing with fury.

Willa's mother and father locked gazes and turned to face Grey in unison.

"No," her father said simply. He reached for his wife's hand and pulled her to her feet to join him. "We won't. In fact, we have obeyed our last command from you, young Mister West. Without Joseph at the helm, we have no interest in remaining with the Big Sky Canyon pack."

The room went silent but for her mother's indignant sniff.

"This seems premature, don't you think?" Grey finally said.

"No. On the contrary, we stayed a week longer than we wanted to."

The alpha pushed his chair backward, away from his desk, and eyed the two of them grimly. "I had hoped you'd give me the opportunity to prove myself. To show you a better way. But I understand and respect your decision, and you will both be missed."

There was no love lost between them, and everyone in the room recognized that lie for what it was, but clearly Grey didn't see the whole picture yet. No worry there, because Willa could tell by the dark glee in her mother's eyes that she was about to clear it up for him.

"Both?" A cruel smile tugged at the corner of Faustine's mouth. "Oh, no, Mr. West. I believe you've miscounted. There are three in our little family."

The room went silent and all of them turned to Willa.

The initial shock in Grey's eyes quickly gave way to sadness and regret. He shook his head slowly and blew out a sigh. "You agree with them, Will?" he asked softly.

She felt for him. She really did. And, over the course of the past week, she'd even found her way to forgiveness of a sort. But she couldn't stay in Big Sky Canyon. Not after everything that had happened. For the past twenty-five years, she'd been subjected to her parents' views on everything from politics to marriage, and had disagreed with pretty much everything they had told her. This time, though, she couldn't dismiss them. They had warned her that the pack would treat her differently now that she'd been jilted by the alpha, and they were right.

More than that, they seemed like they actually cared this time. When Joseph had been imprisoned and Grey and his new mate were announced, her mother had comforted her. Her father had even hugged her, albeit rather stiffly. So when they'd told her they were going to find a new pack, and asked her to join them, she agreed.

Nothing was set in stone. If she hated it, she could leave.

But the way things were right now? All she wanted to do was to get away from here. Away from the furtive, pitying glances, and the not-so furtive whispers, as quickly as possible. She'd make major life decisions later, after she'd had a chance to lick her wounds in private for a while.

"Willa?" Grey called her name again, and she turned her gaze on him. "Is this truly what you want?"

"Don't put that on me, old friend. This isn't about what I want." She flicked a glance at Maggie, who sat beside Grey, her brow wrinkled with concern. "This is about what has to be."

She rolled to her feet and brushed some imaginary lint off her jeans, suddenly desperate to get out of there before the waterworks started. Memories of her and Grey ran through her mind, one after the other.

The two of them romping around in the new Fall leaves as pups, and chasing one another through the trees in the forest, seeing who could leap the furthest. Waking up at the crack of dawn to go on their very first hunt. That time in their teen years where they'd kissed for the first time. It was apparent there was no fiery, passionate spark there, but there was a strong, sweet bond between them that had been enough for Willa.

But apparently not enough for Grey.

"I wish you nothing but success as the new alpha. And I'm sorry it had to come to this."

Maggie stood to join Grey and finally broke her silence. "You will always," she reached out a hand and threaded her fingers with Willa's, "always be welcome here with open arms, should you choose to come back," she murmured softly. Her words were for Willa alone, and she appreciated the gesture. But it was exactly that.

A gesture.

It changed nothing, and the reality was, Willa had to think

of herself right now. She needed to find a place with a new pack where she could start fresh, and out of the shadow of her failure.

"Goodbye, Grey. Maggie."

Her father swept toward the door and held it open, ushering Willa and her mother through.

She almost made it all the way to the car before she started to cry.

Faustine slid a bony arm around her shoulder and patted her gently. "It's all right, darling. It will all be over soon."

Willa nodded, but deep down, she wasn't sure of that. How long did it take before one got over losing everything?

She let her mother lead her to the car and then slid into the back seat. A chill ran over her as her father turned the key in the ignition and she gazed out at the Big Sky land through blurry eyes.

This was really it. She was leaving the only home she'd ever known, and might never come back.

The car ride was long and silent, as they each seemed to be lost in their own thoughts. That was good. The last thing she felt like doing was talking.

As day gave way to night, she fell into a fitful sleep, only awakening hours later when her stomach growled. She looked around blearily and wiped the sleep from her eyes.

"What time is it?"

Her mother kept her gaze locked on the windshield as she answered. "Almost midnight."

Willa tipped her head and eyed her mother's profile in the moonlight. "How much further is it?"

Montana was big, to be sure, but they'd been in the car forever now and they'd be hitting the border if they kept going west.

Faustine's lips pursed and she shot a quick glance as her husband. "Well, actually, you were sleeping so I didn't want to wake you after you'd had such an upsetting evening." She turned and offered Willa a reassuring smile that looked out of place on her thin lips. "The pack that has invited us to stay is an hour in the other direction, but we have to make a stop first."

Willa unfolded her legs that had been tucked beneath her bottom and straightened. A buzz of awareness--and not the good kind--raised the hairs on the back of her neck as she studied Faustine's placid features.

"A stop?"

"Yes, dear. Your father and I haven't just been in talks with this pack we mentioned. What we didn't tell you is that we've managed to secure a private meeting between you and another alpha."

Willa shook her head slowly. "A private meeting? Why would--" She broke off as it hit her. Not a week after her engagement to Grey had been cast aside, her parents were already on the hunt for a replacement.

She could feel her cheeks going hot with the humiliation of it all.

"Mother, I thought you knew my views on this. I agreed to marry Grey because it had been the plan my whole life and I didn't want to dishonor you or the traditions of our pack, but if there was any positive that came from all this, it was that I would get to choose a mate on my own."

She tried to keep her voice steady. They were backward and old-fashioned in their thinking, but they loved her in their way and right now, they were all she had. Giving them the benefit of the doubt was as much for her as it was for them. Surely, they would be able to see it her way this time.

"Oh, my head-in-the-clouds, romantic daughter. I admire your idealism."

Her mother said the words, but they were the furthest thing from sincere. Her parents despised idealism and they viewed romantic love as a weakness. Packs stayed strong by mating their best pups, and that was that.

"You need to understand, Willa. Now, more than ever, if we want to retain our way of life, we have to surround ourselves with like minds. Allies who believe as we do, and want to continue the traditions we've set forth for thousands of years. In order to do that, we need to secure a good match for you. A match that helps us as a family. A match that is about common sense, and pragmatism. Surely you understand that?"

She *understood*, all right.

But that didn't mean she had to agree to it. They needed to get their heads around that as soon as possible, and there was no time like the present.

"I'm not going to marry someone just so that you and father can get ahead politically."

Her father blew out a long sigh and caught her eye in the rearview mirror. "I won't tolerate your disrespect, Willa. Greyson West wronged you. And I promise, he will pay for that slight. But first we need to find some allies. In order to facilitate that, you need to get on board and do what you're told."

A sense of dread crawled up the back of her neck as his words hit home.

"What do you mean, Grey will pay? His father is imprisoned and half-mad. We left the pack, and I doubt we'll be the only ones to defect."

He'd looked so sad...so tired behind that big desk.

She shoved aside her sympathy and pushed forward. "He's paid enough for his perceived crimes. I don't want to be there anymore, but I don't want to fight or be angry anymore either. I just want to find a home and move on with my life."

The air was tense, and she braced herself for an argument. But her father just reached down and clicked on the radio without responding.

It would've been nice if they could talk things through like a real family for once.

Maybe this was a mistake, after all. Maybe she should've given it a little more time before walking away. This wasn't the first scandal to hit their pack, and it wouldn't be the last. Maybe in a few weeks, the gossip would die down, and she could go back.

Even Maggie had said she would be welcome.

Willa was still deep in thought when the car finally slowed.

They'd been on a steady incline up the side of a mountain for the past hour now, and her father pulled off onto a scenic overlook.

He unbuckled his seatbelt and turned to face her. "Let's stretch our legs, and have a bite to eat here. We'll discuss your meeting once our stomachs are full."

She didn't have high hopes for that discussion, but at least he was agreeing to listen. And, after being cooped up all this time, she could certainly use the stretch. Wolves didn't do well in close spaces for long periods, and she was starting to get twitchy.

Her parents climbed out of the car and Willa followed suit, taking a moment to grab the knapsack of food she'd packed. She'd barely taken a step onto the gravel when a loud roar sounded above her head. Before she could even process what was happening, the sky was lit with fire.

But it was what the fire illuminated that had the knapsack falling from her limp fingers to the ground.

"Holy mother of god, what is it?" she whispered, her heart pounding so hard, she could hear it, even over the beating of massive, black wings. The shape of the beast grew closer as it swooped low, just above her now.

Its poison green gaze locked with hers and she scrambled backward in terror.

Dimly, she heard the car doors slam and the engine start as a single word raced through her mind over and over again.

Dragon.

Get the rest of Coercion now, free in Kindle Unlimited!

ALSO BY CHRISTINE GAEL

Maeve's Girls

Finding Tomorrow

Finding Home

Finding Peace

Sign up for Christine's mailing list to get exclusive content and insider info on upcoming releases!

Manufactured by Amazon.ca
Bolton, ON